Waters of Change

The Unspoken Heart Series

Amy Astorga

Waters of Change
The Unspoken Heart Series

Copyright © March 16, 2015 by Amy Astorga

ISBN 9780996156202

Interior design by Kimberly Martin of Jera Publishing
Cover design by Story Graphix Plus
Copy editing by Natalie Jean Astorga and Emmanuel Alonso Astorga

For my father who dared me to dream,
and my husband who knew that I could.

"The heart is deceitful above all things, and desperately wicked: who can know it?"

Jeremiah 17:9 NKJV

Chapter One

"Gwen, are you awake?" My father tapped out a rhythm on my bedroom door and paused.

I lifted my head from my pillow and slowly opened my eyes. Morning light streamed through my sheer curtains and bathed my room in a soft pink glow. They fluttered about as a cool breeze blew, casting a series of shadows that played across the walls. I glanced at my alarm clock that hid behind magazines and gave a groggy yawn. The party wasn't only an emotional roller-coaster—it left me completely exhausted.

My father said something to someone in the hallway and knocked again. "Are you awake, sweetheart?" He opened my door to a crack and peered inside.

"Hey, Dad. I'm awake."

A muffled beep came from my nightstand, and I reached to open its drawer. My hand froze in midair as an object caught my eye. A diamond ring reflected a beam of light in its prism and twinkled. An image of Ryan bending down on one knee flashed through my mind. His blue eyes danced with excitement while he reached into his back pocket and pulled out a small black box.

"Gwendolyn Ann Hart, will you marry me?"

I fumbled for the beeping cell phone and opened it. Emma had called three times and left a message. "You can come in," I muttered, turning it off with a sigh.

I leaned back on my pillows and pulled my comforter to my chest. I wasn't surprised to see Emma had called. She probably had a prick of conscience and was frantically trying to backpedal. Her attitude at the party was painfully hard to accept. Anyone with half a heart would feel the need to apologize—especially someone who called herself my best friend.

My father walked into my room and looked down at a pile of clothes on the floor. "Honey, Emma's here to see you." He looked over his shoulder and closed the door behind himself. "Is everything okay with you guys? She seems kind of tense." He tucked his collared shirt into his slacks and slung a tie around his neck.

"Yeah, I guess so. You know, the same old drama. Why?"

"Dads just know these things. And your mother tells me she's been pretty grumpy these last few weeks."

I nodded my head at the grossly understated comment and chuckled. Emma wasn't only grumpy, but egocentric, jealous, and vain. She wasn't even a shadow of who she used to be. My flourishing relationship with Ryan only magnified her lack of a boyfriend. Instead of valuing our friendship and embracing our differences, she found every opportunity to single me out. Weekends and parties at the beach served as reminders of our incompatibility. They proved we were going our separate ways. In a strange way, our growing separation gave me peace. That was until she showed up.

"What time did you come home last night? I didn't hear you get in." He knotted the top of his tie and tucked the end into his pants. He paused from smoothing his shirt to look for my response. I glanced down at my hand and quickly hid it under my sheet. I had gotten home late and was unable to share Ryan's proposal. I wanted the announcement to be memorable and special, not discovered accidentally.

"Oh, I think it was around eleven-thirty or so. Give or take," I said nonchalantly, waving my other hand.

"Well, next time make sure to poke your head in our room and let us know you're in. It saves your mother the heartache of wondering where you are." He leaned over to give me a kiss on my cheek. "Play nice, sweetheart. I'll tell Emma to come in now." He gave me a parting hug and slipped into the hall.

I held my breath and listened as inaudible talking was exchanged. A few seconds later and Emma appeared in the doorway. She entered my room cautiously as if she knew her presence was intrusive. She slipped off her shoes at the foot of my bed and slowly took a seat. I didn't say anything to her at first. Partly because I was gauging the situation, partly because I had nothing to say. She folded her long, slender legs under herself and stared at her hands in her lap.

"I'm sorry," she said in a small voice.

There was a long moment of silence before I answered. "Okay."

"No, really Gwen. I'm sorry. I was wrong for getting angry with you."

I avoided her eyes and studied the tiny rose pattern in my bedspread.

"I didn't have it together last night. The beach is a pretty depressing place if you don't have someone to share it with. You were hanging out with Ryan, and I guess I felt left out. Everyone either went to prom or was coming back from it. You know how badly I wanted to go. I was reduced to sitting on a filthy blanket watching Joey down power drinks." She tugged on a thin strand of her brown hair and examined it in the light. "I wish you could understand the letdown in that. I don't know, when you mentioned I should consider counseling, I felt insulted. You don't really think I need help, do you?"

She waited for me to look up, but I continued to stare at my bed. The more she talked and made excuses for her behavior, the more I wished for her to disappear.

"I didn't mention counseling for one isolated incident," I said, finally meeting her eyes. "I can understand your disappointment in missing prom. That's not what I'm concerned about. You've been depressed for a really long time now. And I've done everything I can to make you feel included. You're always so negative when it comes to Ryan's and my relationship. We're together and will be for a while. I don't think you're happy with that." My right hand buttoned the top of my pajamas while my left hand remained firmly planted under my sheet. I didn't feel like receiving fake accolades so early in the morning.

"You know, you're right," she said, sweeping her hair out of her eyes. "I have been rude. And maybe even a little jealous. But can you blame me for that? Who wouldn't want what you have?" Her attention drifted toward a collage of pictures mounted on a corkboard.

Suddenly, her countenance changed, and she sat up very tall. Her face washed pink with emotion as she struggled to conceal a creeping smile. "But you know what?" she teased, biting her lower lip. "There was a reason why I didn't go to prom. I was supposed to be at that party. Something really awesome happened last night, and I've waited all morning to tell you . . ." She paused to add suspense. "I met him!"

I scanned her face that glowed with excitement and looked the other way. It was selfish of her to dismiss my pain so quickly. Any remorse she felt for her insolent behavior had all at once vanished in an opportunity to brag. Naturally, I wanted to inquire about her romance and sweep it all under the rug. I also wanted to rip the bandage off and dig deeper into the wound. The better part of my brain told my mouth to smile.

"Really?"

"Yes! I met him. The one. The guy you've been telling me to wait for. My Mister Right." She reached across the bed and shook my arm with a squeal. "And he's gorgeous. I wish you could've met him. If I knew he was there, I would've at least brushed the sand out of my hair. You know how tangled it gets when we go to the beach. He said I looked great, but I was wearing Joey's sweatshirt of all things." She poked fun at her appearance and burst into laughter.

I covered my mouth with my hand and tried to suppress a chuckle. I wanted to be happy for my friend. For the first time in months, she appeared to have a genuine smile. It felt good to see her sitting on the edge of my bed, laughing and enjoying life. It felt like old times.

"That's great, Em. Tell me what happened."

"Well, after you and I had that argument, I took a walk by the tide pools where I could think about life and stuff. Then, this gorgeous guy appeared out of the middle of nowhere. He was in the water, and from what I could see, he was a surfer or something. He was toned. I mean, like, bodybuilder toned. If only you could've seen his arms. I'll tell you, they put Ryan's to shame."

I smiled at the tease.

"Anyways, we started talking and wound up having a full-blown conversation. He told me he waited his whole life to meet me. Can you believe that? And then, he gave me this . . ." She lowered the neckline of her shirt to reveal a pearl necklace. "Check it out. It looks even more special up close." She unclasped the back of her prize and handed it to me.

I held it up to a shaft of light and gasped. It was the prettiest piece of jewelry I've ever seen. All the pearls were different and had an organic look to them. Some were small while others were quite large. They each varied in color, ranging from pale pink to cream. But the beauty didn't come from the pearls so much as what they were strung with. Very thin strands of fishing line were intricately woven, connecting each pearl together in an artwork of brilliance.

"Wow! This is beautiful, Em. Look how each pearl is tied together in a perfect row. Someone must've taken a long time to make this." I held it up to examine it again. "And what an interesting material to string it with. I've seen pearls on gold or silver chains, but never on fishing line. You would think it would make it look cheap, but it doesn't. It gives it an interesting touch." I handed her back her treasure.

"I know. It looks different, doesn't it?" she boasted, putting it back on. "It's not like the junk you find people selling down by the beach. They sell glass beads strung with hemp, but this . . ." She pushed out her chest to look at her reflection in the mirror. "And my mom taught me once how to tell real pearls from fake ones."

"Yeah? How?"

"You take the pearl in question and lightly rub your tooth against its surface. If it feels smooth, it's a fake. If it has a grainy feel to it, it's real. Well, I checked all of them, and they're all real."

My hand felt the ring circling my finger. I wanted Emma to share in my moment, too.

"And you know what the best part of the whole night was?" she continued.

"Yeah? What's that?"

"He told me he loved me."

"He told you what?" I asked, unsure if I heard correctly.

"He told me he loved me," she repeated proudly.

"He told you he loved you?"

I felt my brow furrow. Love isn't something you tell someone after knowing them for a night. Such words might be uttered at a party with ulterior motives, but never to be taken seriously. Emma had to see this was a major red flag.

A costly piece of jewelry given by a stranger was a stretch, but love—that was just plain creepy.

She turned from her reflection and frowned. "Is there something wrong with that?"

"Well, yeah, kind of. He doesn't even know you. You guys just met, right? Don't you find that kind of odd?"

"I actually thought it was romantic. You see it all the time in movies. The guy notices the girl across the room. They lock eyes and fall in love. I don't see anything wrong with that." She pulled up the collar of her shirt as if to shield her necklace from our conversation.

"I'm not trying to offend you. I'm really not. It just sounds like this guy is moving pretty fast. Love is a strong word to use when you've just met someone. Don't you think? Why not give it some time before you give your heart away? I don't want to see you get hurt."

She gave me a dirty look and walked to the back of the room. She pushed away the curtain that fluttered around the window and spun around. "And who made you a relationship expert all of a sudden? Do you think you know everything there is to know about guys? Your relationship history involves, um . . . how many? One. And from last I saw, Ryan was crushing on Samantha at the party. Could it be that the tables have turned, and now you're feeling a little jealous yourself?"

My eyes locked with hers and narrowed. The audacity of her comment was unbelievable.

"Emma, why did you come here this morning? Why did you call? I don't even have to listen to the voicemail to get my answer. You didn't call to apologize, but to brag."

She opened her mouth to answer, but I cut her off before she could respond.

"You're a very selfish person. You've been treating me like trash for a while now, and quite frankly, I'm finished with it. I think it's time you go home."

My blunt response caught her by surprise. Her wide eyes scanned my face for sincerity.

"What?"

"Leave. And don't come back until you get over yourself." I struggled to control my rapid breathing as I pointed to the door. She just stared at me in shock.

"Are you serious?"

I nodded my head in unwavering certainty and clutched my hands together in a tight ball. It felt like every nerve ending in my body was involuntarily twitching. I resisted the urge to stop her as she sputtered something indiscernible and turned to find her purse. She gave me one last confused look before turning on her heel and walking out the door.

I lay there motionless as her car door slammed, and she sped down the street. My words hung in the air and repeated themselves over and over.

"Leave. And don't come back until you get over yourself." My outstretched finger pointed her to the door. Her look of rage, followed by confusion.

I was alone with my thoughts, yet I was unable to think past the last five minutes. I remained in my bed and waited as I tried to process a morning that continued to march on. A neighbor's lawn mower started, and a dog barked in response. The trash truck came down our street and stopped briefly before noisily driving off. A gust of wind blew through my open window, and several papers flew from my desk. My room was starting to feel warm and sticky, marking the beginning of another hot afternoon.

I took a deep breath and pulled off the sweaty sheets that twisted around my waist. I needed to go somewhere and get my mind off things. Maybe I could look at wedding dresses, I thought with a smile. I brushed through the tangles in my long, blonde hair and pulled it back in a high ponytail. As I studied my reflection in my dresser mirror, an image of Emma flashed through my mind. Her face was proud as she stuck out her chest to flaunt her precious necklace. I shook my head and turned to grab my car keys.

Who gives someone so much when they hardly know who they are?

Chapter Two

I shot up in bed.

A loud vibration sounded from my nightstand, causing my skin to crawl with goosebumps. I glanced at my alarm clock and reached to grab my cell phone. It was three forty-six in the morning. My mind began to race as Emma's house number registered on the caller's identification.

"Hello?"

"Gwendolyn? I'm sorry for waking you, but is Emma there? I'd like to speak to her, if that's okay." Emma's mom sounded panicked.

"Emma? I'm sorry, Ms. Stineburt, but Emma isn't here."

"She isn't? Well, where is she? She never called me back, so I figured she spent the night at your house. I just wanted to double check and make sure. What time did your movie end?"

"Movie?"

"Yes, the movie," she repeated, sounding impatient. "The one you and Emma were supposed to watch tonight. She said she would be out late, but you know how I feel about her coming home past twelve."

My mind groped for answers while I tried to piece together what she was saying. None of it made any sense.

"I'm sorry, but I haven't talked to Emma since yesterday morning. I don't know what you're talking about. We didn't have plans to see a movie tonight."

"What do you mean you didn't have plans? She told me . . ." Her voice trailed to silence.

"Did you try calling her cell phone?"

"Yes, of course, I tried calling her at least a dozen times." She let out her breath in an angry hiss. "That's why I'm calling you. What I don't understand is why she would lie about having plans with you. She has nothing to hide, right?"

I met him! The one. The guy you've been telling me to wait for. My Mister Right.

"No. I don't think she has anything to hide," I lied, not wanting to get involved. "I'll let you know if I hear from her, though."

"Yes. Will you do that for me? Tell her she's in real trouble over here. I won't allow for dishonesty in this house."

"I'll do that, Ms. Stineburt. I'm very sorry you're having trouble."

"I'm sorry for waking you. Please let me know if you hear from her."

"I will. Goodnight."

I hung up from our call and watched as the pictures slowly rotated on my home screen. Something wasn't right. And it wasn't the obvious deception between Emma and her mother. Their relationship had always been strained since her parents' divorce. Her mother had become strict and overbearing, relying heavily on discipline and structure to compensate for the loss of control in her personal life. Her micromanaging destroyed her relationship with her daughter, making communication of difficult matters nearly impossible. Clearly, Emma had plans to see someone whom her mother would disapprove of, and she felt the need to deceive her to do so. But it wasn't the lie that set me on edge, so much as the disregard to follow it through. Why would she tell her mother she would be home after a movie if she was planning to be out all night? A simple call explaining that she was spending the night at my house would've covered her tracks. Surely she knew her mother would look for her and call me. And why wasn't she answering her phone? Not to mention, it was totally out of character for Emma to be out past twelve in the first place. I nervously flipped through the numbers in my cell phone and tried to piece the puzzle together.

She was with him.

That much I knew for sure. Only lust would make someone do such foolish things. It was a careless choice to spend the night with a complete stranger. She was putting herself in a vulnerable, possibly dangerous position. I wrestled within myself not to care. She could make decisions for herself. She didn't need my approval, or lack thereof, of her romantic affairs. If she was put in a position of compromise that was ultimately her choice. Still, I felt a sense of responsibility for her well-being. I rested my head on my damp pillow and flipped it to its drier side. She was once my best friend. I would want someone to be the voice of reason if I were on the cusp of insanity.

I picked up my phone without further hesitation and called her number. The phone rang several times before her giddy voice announced to leave a message.

"Uh . . . hey, Em. It's me, Gwen. I'm sorry for calling you so late. I hope this isn't a bad time or anything. Listen, I'm sorry for yesterday. I didn't mean to insult you. I was just really concerned for your well-being. Maybe too much. I'll admit to that. I just want to see you happy. And well, just make sure you think with your head and not with your heart. Sometimes it can get us into trouble. I'm here for you if you need anything. Okay? I hope to talk to you soon."

I hung up with a yawn and set the phone on my nightstand. For the remainder of the night, I waited for a call that would never arrive.

***

The following three weeks went by in a painful blur. Emma never came home. Puzzlement and anger at her absence quickly turned to panic and fear. It seemed as though the whole city of GlenPoint was rocked to the core by her disappearance. Posters were hung on street corners and in coffee shops. The police investigation became extensive, involving public questioning and bloodhound searches. Even our school had an assembly discussing date safety and the buddy system. People from all over claimed to be her concerned friend just to share in a piece of the limelight. Graduation came and went. Ryan attended and said they announced her name, followed by a moment of silence to respect her disappearance. I chose not to go and have my diploma mailed. My parents were disappointed with my decision, but they understood my withdrawal. They grappled with fears of the unknown, putting locks on windows that were once left open and strict curfews on ones that were once relaxed. I was forbidden to be out past eleven, regardless of who I was with or where we were going. Eventually, the stress of the situation put a burden on my relationship with Ryan. His reserves of sympathy ran dry as every conversation was dominated by Emma in some way. She had become the center focus of my life, and he couldn't understand why. He wanted me to be excited about our future and to plan for our big day, but I couldn't see past the present.

On the three-week anniversary of Emma's disappearance, the town's sheriff called for a mandatory meeting at her house. It took every ounce of strength for me to get dressed and not hide my head under my pillow. I threw on a sweatshirt and an old pair of jeans and answered the knocking at the door.

"Hey," I mumbled, squinting from the flood of morning light.

"Hey," Ryan greeted quietly. His eyes dropped from my face to the floor while he waited for me to say something. After a few seconds of awkward silence, he coughed and asked, "Are you ready to go to that meeting?"

"Yeah. I'm ready."

"Okay. Well . . . let's go then." He stretched out his hand for mine and silently led me to his truck. I threw my hood over my tangled hair and slid into the front seat. I wanted to run back to my room and lock the door behind me, but the start of his engine finalized my decision. I looked out my window and sighed in painful surrender.

"I wish we didn't have to go to this thing," he muttered, pulling out of my driveway. "But Officer Black really gave us no choice, did he? I guess they found something at the beach that pertained to the case and wanted to pick our brains. Like we have any involvement anyways." He stopped at a red light and turned to give me his full attention. His eyes scanned my appearance and became sorrowful.

"Who's we?" I questioned, avoiding his prying stare.

"What do you mean?"

"You said the word 'we'. Are there other people coming today?" I pointed to the light that turned green.

"Well, yeah, I think so. From what I understand, Joey and Jessica were asked to attend. Why?"

"Jessica? Why is she coming? She doesn't even know Emma. And Joey? Come on. Are you serious?"

"Hey, babe, I wasn't the one who invited them. I don't know why they're coming. You know how people talk. Everyone has something to say now that she's gone. I'm sure Jessica is just one of the many who claim to be Emma's friend." He reached across the seat and covered my hand with his. "But you don't have anything to worry about. Everybody knows you were Emma's true best friend."

I pulled his hand off mine and flung it across the car. "Do you think that's what this is all about? I don't care if people know I was Emma's best friend or not. This isn't some popularity contest I'm trying to win. What bothers me is that ever since she went missing, everybody suddenly cares about her. She's more popular now than when she was around."

Ryan turned the corner of her street and pulled off to the side of the road. He reached to grasp my arm, but I shrugged him away.

"Babe, look at me. Look at me! I'm not the bad guy here, okay? I'm only trying to help. I may not have all the right answers, but you aren't making things any easier. It's like there's no winning with you anymore. I say the wrong thing, and you come out of your corner swinging. I'm trying. I'm trying really hard. Give me a little credit here." He gave an irritated groan and raked his hand through his sandy brown hair. Every muscle under his tight shirt bulged with tension. His fist clenched the steering wheel so hard his knuckles turned white.

The car became silent. I was wrong for treating him with indifference, and I knew it. In my darkest moments of grief, Ryan receded into the shadows. But not of his own doing. I pushed him away because I couldn't process my emotions. There was nothing he could say or do that would bring my friend back. His responses were flippant and sounded trite in comparison to the depths of my sorrow. And all the while, he remained clueless to any wrongdoing. My frustration slowly vanished as I took in his drained countenance. Although he lacked in the department of satisfactory consolation, he was doing the best he could.

"I'm so sorry," I said, smoothing the length of his arm. "I really am. I shouldn't expect some textbook answer from you every time I share my problems. It's not your fault. It's mine. We're going to get through this. For better or for worse, right?" I lifted his fist to my lips and kissed it.

"That's if you still want me," he muttered, pulling away from the curb.

For the rest of the car ride, we drove in silence as we made our way to the dreaded meeting.

The room was hot and stuffy, and for the exception of three small floor fans blowing hot air around, the atmosphere was near unbearable. I took my sweatshirt off and tied it around my waist as we walked through Emma's front door. I looked around the crowded room, barely recognizing it from the visits I'd made in the past. The house was a complete mess. Dust and take-out boxes covered every flat surface they could find. A stack of dirty dishes was piled high in the kitchen sink, and a wastebasket overflowed with trash nearby. The air smelled thick of stale cigarettes, revealing a rediscovered habit that Ms. Stineburt supposedly abandoned.

Ryan and I entered the small circle of guests and slowly took our seats. Joey smoothed back his hot pink hair and grimaced, looking as though he couldn't endure another second. Jessica, who was seated next to Joey, hardly glanced up from inspecting her polished nails. Her black hair was spiked high in the front and fell to her waist in the back. Her cream-colored lace dress was cut just short enough to reveal a tattoo of a bat peeking through her fishnet stockings. She made eye contact with me and smirked before eyeing her nails again.

"Gwendolyn! Ryan! Glad you could make it," Officer Black announced from the back of the room. He stepped into the middle of the circle and waited as Ms. Stineburt and her ex-husband, Burt, slowly appeared in the kitchen doorway.

"Great. We're all here now. Are we ready to begin?" He looked around the room for a response and received none. "Okay. Well, I want to thank you all for coming here this morning. I know it's a Saturday and it's early, so I'll make it brief. It's been three weeks since Emma's disappearance. Our team has been working hard on this case, and we think we may have some interesting leads. But we still need some more information. I chose you four to come here today because you were the ones who knew Emma the best. I need you to share any insights you may have pertaining to her disappearance. This can be information about her as a person, or maybe something she's mentioned in the past. Anything that would help us get some answers. Bear in mind, this isn't the time for gossip. Your information needs to be as factual as it is helpful. Now, I'm going to start with you, Joey, and let's go around the room in a clockwise direction." His radio squawked loudly, and he reached to his belt to turn it off. He opened his pad of paper and stared at him intently.

Joey looked around the room, wide-eyed with confusion. "I don't know why I'm here, Officer. I didn't even know Emma. We shared fifth-period English class, and I sat behind her. But we never talked. Ryan and Gwen tried to set me up with her a few weeks back. But that's about it." He gave Ryan a dirty look, who looked like he wanted to laugh. He then looked back at the policeman and shrugged his shoulders. "I'm sorry. But I really don't know why I'm here."

"You're here because it was reported to me that you dated Emma for a period of time," the officer answered, not looking up from his notebook.

At that moment, it appeared to take all of Joey's inner strength to keep himself from laughing. "No. I don't know who told you that. Like I said before, Ryan and Gwen tried to set us up. I refused. She wasn't my type." His eyes shot back at Ryan in aggravation.

"Okay, Joey, okay," the officer interrupted. "I'm sorry for the misunderstanding. I still want you to stay here and listen to what everybody else has to say. Perhaps something will come to mind." He smoothed his broad mustache and shifted his focus to Jessica.

She lifted from lacing one of her knee-high leather boots and giggled. "Oh. Is it my turn?"

"Yes."

"Okay. Hi, everyone." She gave a small wave. "All I can say about Emma is that she was depressed. Like, really depressed. She was always complaining about her breakouts and unmanageable hair. And I don't know for sure, but I think she was taking diet pills. They could've been vitamins, but I took a diet pill one time, and it looked just like the ones she was taking. She told me once that she wanted to lose weight, so it only makes sense that they were—"

"Remember, only factual information, Jessica. I need to know only the facts. We don't have time to chase any rabbit trails. But you said she was depressed. Is that right?" He clicked his pen against his chin and began writing something in his book.

"Yes, she was. Every time I spoke with her, she had something negative to say." She took a strand of hair and curled it around her finger.

"And did you ever notice any markings on her skin? Or talks of hurting herself? Anything like that?"

"No. She wasn't that kind of depressed. Just . . ."

"Just bummed out about the average teenage troubles," he finished with a nod.

"Right. That kind of depressed."

"Okay, good. Is there anything else you would like to add?"

"Nope. That's it. I'm just really glad I can help you, Officer. And if you need me for anything else, please let me know." She fluttered her eyelashes and popped a stick of gum in her mouth. I gave her a look of repulsion and turned to face Ryan.

"Ryan, what about you?" The officer peered over his notebook.

For a pensive moment, Ryan studied his folded hands. "Emma was a really cool person." He glanced at her parents. "I always saw her as the little sister I never had. She had a pretty good sense of humor, too. Up until the last year or so, I could make her laugh about anything. And I can vouch for what Jessica said about her being depressed. After a while, she just stopped joking around and stuff. I think she was jealous of Gwen's and my relationship, for whatever reason. Like, she would get ticked when Gwen and I were alone. I think she felt left out. I don't know. The last time I saw her, we were all together at the beach, and she was totally bummed about missing prom. At least that's what I think. And I don't know for sure, but I wouldn't completely rule out suicide. The thought that she may have done something to herself has crossed my mind a few times."

From the corner of my eye, I saw Emma's mom begin to pace in the doorway.

"And why would you suggest that? Have you ever heard or seen anything that would concern you?"

"No. Just a bad feeling, that's all. When someone's depressed for a long time, something has to give. Right?"

"Have any of you ever mentioned to Emma that she should seek help? A counselor or a parent? Perhaps another close friend?" The officer looked around the room, and everyone shook their heads in unison.

"I have," I said quietly. I lifted my head and met the policeman's penetrating stare. "I told her she should talk to the school counselor on the night she missed prom."

"And what did she say when you suggested that?"

"She got offended because I thought she was so unstable. She was angry and left the party."

"And was that the Friday before she disappeared?"

"Yes."

"And was that the last time you spoke to Emma?"

"No."

He stood abruptly and retrieved a folder fastened to his clipboard. He studied it briefly and walked the length of the room.

"Well, as I stated before, we found some new leads that pertain to the case. Two days ago, a little boy was playing at the beach and dug up Emma's cell phone. It was buried about six inches from the shoreline out by GlenPoint Pier. We were able to salvage the cell phone's memory chip and extract every call that came in and went out. Nothing seemed out of the ordinary. Nothing except one call. The night that

Emma was in question, you, Gwendolyn, made a phone call at four-ten in the morning. You stated in your message, and I quote, 'I just want to see you happy. And well, just make sure you think with your head and not with your heart. Sometimes it can get us into trouble.' Do you remember making that phone call?"

I felt my face drain of color. In the wake of my sorrow and self-pity, I had completely overlooked reporting the vital information I knew.

"Yes. I remember making that call."

"Well, can you please explain what trouble you foresaw her getting into on the night she disappeared?"

Everyone's eyes hungrily looked to mine for answers. The figure that was in the back of the room stopped pacing and stepped further in to listen.

"Yes, I can explain. The morning after we all met at the beach, Emma came by my house and told me she met someone the night before. He gave her a pearl necklace and told her he loved her. I warned her that he was moving pretty fast and told her to take it slow. She became very upset with my advice and stormed out of my house. That was the last time I saw her. Emma's mom called me that night and said she never came home. I thought she might've been with him, so I called to tell her not to think with her heart. I didn't want to see her get hurt."

"You little liar!" Ms. Stineburt screamed. "You told me Emma had nothing to hide! You knew she could've been with some strange man this whole time?"

Jessica gasped as she marched to our circle of chairs and stopped within inches of my face. I flinched from her outstretched finger, expecting to be smacked across the face in an outpouring of wrath.

"You knew this whole time and didn't say anything? Why? Are you covering up for her?" Deep furrows etched around her black sunken eyes. She pulled a cigarette from her back pocket and lit it, taking a long, deep drag.

"Come on, Beth! Knock it off. She's just a kid. And why do you have to smoke those darn things anyways?" Burt stepped out from the kitchen.

The officer stood from his chair and crossed the room in a few long strides. "Beth! Please respect the meeting. I know you may not like some of the answers you're hearing. But remember, we're all here for the same purpose. I need you to take a seat and not interrupt again."

She glared at me one last time before taking another puff of her cigarette. She turned and followed him back to the kitchen. They exchanged a few tense words before he reappeared and slid his chair to face mine. His eyes studied mine carefully.

"Gwendolyn, how are you feeling?"

"I wasn't covering for her," I answered weakly. "I just didn't think about it, that's all. The night you called me, Ms. Stineburt, I should've told you about him. But I felt it wasn't my place to say anything. I didn't know Emma wouldn't come home. And, to be quite honest with you, it never occurred to me to say anything after she went missing. I can't explain why. It's like the information was locked in my brain somehow."

"Well, that doesn't matter now. Does it?" The officer turned to look at Ms. Stineburt. "What's important is that we know now. Gwendolyn, did she say anything else to you about him? A description or a name? Anything like that?"

"She said he was handsome with a nice build. That's about it. She didn't mention his name."

"And you said he gave her a pearl necklace? Were you able to see it?"

"Yes, I did. And it looked different. Handmade, yet very expensive. Perhaps he bought it from a local vendor at the pier? I don't know."

"And what about after? Did she mention any future dates with this man?" He scribbled wildly in his notepad.

"No. No, she didn't. She stopped talking to me the second she saw I didn't approve of him. I've never been afraid to tell Emma the truth about things. And I've always looked out for her best interests. Even when she didn't want me to." I looked to see if Ms. Stineburt acknowledged my concern, but she refused to make eye contact. The tip of her cigarette glowed red as she took in a deep breath and blew the smoke out through her nostrils. Her eyes looked at her ex-husband's in frustration.

"Well, we have a lot of work ahead of us here." The officer sighed and looked around the room. "But I need you six to be my eyes and ears. If you discover any significant information relating to this case, please don't hesitate to call. I'm leaving you with the police department's business card. On the back of the card is my cell phone number. Now, I mean it! If you see or hear anything, you need to call me as soon as possible. Time is of the essence here, and there's none to waste. Let's bring their baby girl home." He clapped his folder closed and adjusted his heavy belt of equipment.

Ryan smoothed my hand and waited for the officer to leave the room.

"Wow. That was rough, wasn't it? Emma's mom really had it out for you."

I could only nod my head in agreement. Emma's mom needed vengeance. And who could blame her? Her world had been shattered, and she needed someone to blame. At that moment, I wondered how many regrets were torturing her soul. How many nights did she toss in bed, wishing she could recapture a relationship with her daughter that never existed? She would seek a rest from her problems—a rest that would never come. All at once, I looked at Ms. Stineburt with an unexpected sense of pity. Yes, my trespasses created the perfect scapegoat. But her trespasses ran even deeper.

"Are you ready to leave now?" Ryan asked, standing to his feet.

A sudden commotion sounded from the kitchen as Emma's mother fell to the floor, wailing loudly and beating her chest with her fists.

"Yes. I'm ready to leave."

Chapter Three

I needed to drive. I needed to bleed my mind of every thought and of every person pushing behind that thought. I made a list of who I wanted to forget, and I did so. All pain in my life was to be voided and removed.

I needed to reclaim my control.

I rounded the corner of the highway and punched my car into second. Discouragement waited for its invitation. It repeatedly knocked on the door of my heart, hoping to disarm me and gain total surrender. I carefully watched for any intruders as I examined my walls for repair. If a thought of Emma slipped in, I simply pushed it out. If Ryan's tired expression flashed through my memory, I turned up the music louder. I stepped on the gas a little harder as an image of Ms. Stineburt fell to the floor. Some battles weren't fought with flesh and blood but were waged within the spirit and mind.

For an hour, I drove up the coast of GlenPoint and wrestled with the demons of my soul. I was discouraged and clouded, and by the time I focused on the road before me, I discovered I no longer knew where I was. The fast-paced four-lane highway merged into two as it climbed the steep mountainside. I unwillingly exited the city limits and slowed my car with caution. The last thing I needed was to get lost and have to call my overprotective parents for directions.

I spotted a scenic turnout at the side of the road and pulled into the empty parking space. The opportunity to rest was a welcomed relief from the stressful drive. I turned my idling car off and closed my eyes in despair.

If there were only a way to make it all disappear.

If only I could press some magic button in my head and make all my worries vanish from memory. I could revert to my life when my biggest problems could be resolved with a bowlful of ice cream and a good movie. But, of course, I knew the answers were never that easy.

I opened my eyes and was pulled from my introspective drowning. Pink and gold painted a sky that was stretched above a sea of sapphire. The longer I stared at the ocean before me, the more I was drawn to its mysterious splendor. I rolled down my window and took in a deep breath of the salty sea air. With each breath I took, my heart was cleansed of all anguish, until all that remained was tranquility and the ocean outside. A compelling urge to visit the beach suddenly called me from below. The desire was so strong that I literally wanted to thrust myself off the cliff and become one with the thundering waves.

Go to the beach.

I unquestioningly opened my car door and stepped out into the lot. My eyes were drawn to a walking trail that descended the mountainside. I walked to the edge of the cliff and peered over the steep drop. The passageway was more difficult than I had expected, winding through rocky terrain that led to the beach's shore.

I slowly walked back to my car and contemplated my next move. Surely a little stroll wouldn't hurt. I was tense from the drive and needed a place to think. If I hurried, I could take a quick look around and make it back before dark. Still, I didn't want to lose track of time and get stranded in an area I was unfamiliar with.

Go to the beach.

My compulsions took over, and I followed the foreboding path.

The hike proved to be quite challenging. Its narrow pathway twisted through a densely wooded area, which at times was blocked off by low-hanging tree branches and shrubbery. I pulled several leaves out of my hair and stopped to catch my breath. I didn't expect the walk to be so difficult. I questioned within myself why I continued to advance through it. Common sense told me to turn around while I still had light. The pathway would become dangerous without proper visibility. If I left now, I still had time. But the ocean's captivating presence beckoned for me to press forward. I took one last look at the choice behind me and crossed onto the vacant shore.

I slipped off my shoes that burdened my feet and slung them over one shoulder. As soon as my foot made contact with the sand, I felt a change begin. I couldn't explain what it was or why it was there. Perhaps it was the roar of the waves that seemed to be getting louder? Or maybe it was the smell of brine that intoxicated my soul? Or was it the rocky path that turned to silk beneath my feet? Whatever it was, I knew I wasn't the same. It was as if my senses were awakening, fine-tuning somehow, with an odd yet familiar intensity.

I took a few steps toward the sparkling water and stopped to take it in. It didn't look any different. The dark blue waves mounted to foamy white peaks and spilled across the sand. Its movement was the same. Its color was the same. All appeared to be usual. All except me.

What was wrong with me?

A massive wave thundered hard against the shore, surging a blanket of foam that spread across my feet. I looked down at my jeans that dragged in the water and followed the receding wave. My skin broke in gooseflesh as another wave struck and water rose to my shins. I smoothed back my hair that blew across my face and took a few more steps. Another wave collided before me. I followed without question. The breath I held grew hot in my lungs while I waited for the ocean to respond.

I waited . . .

Then . . .

Nothing.

As quickly as the moment came, it vanished, leaving me knee-deep in the ocean's current, cold and trembling. I looked down at my arms that reached for the water and slowly lowered them to my sides.

What was I doing?

A large wave suddenly crashed against me, planting me face-first into a wall of icy surf. I lifted my head and gasped as a stinging mouthful of saltwater flooded the back of my throat. I sputtered out the gritty liquid and frantically pulled up from the ocean's sucking tug. The powerful surf retracted briefly, allowing for my knees to steady on the shifting sand. With long, forceful strides, I dragged my seemingly lame body to the shore and plopped down on the ground.

I tilted my head back and let out an exhausted groan. Every muscle in my body ached from the unexpected swim. I felt so tired that I wanted to curl up in a ball and sleep the rest of the night on the beach. I moved my leg from an incoming wave and tried my best not to panic.

What just happened?

Why was I in the water? Why was my memory so vague? It was like I woke up from a dream and was scrambling to put the pieces together. I remembered wanting to take a walk. My mind was overworked, and I needed a place to think. But the ocean's characteristics were unnaturally different. And I was different, too. Why?

A gust of wind cooled the wet clothes that were plastered against my skin. I hugged my sides in a failed attempt to get warm and let out a shaky breath. How did I go from being dry and comfortable in my car to drenched and exhausted on the beach? What was wrong with my rational judgment? It was such a poor decision to go exploring so late in the day. I glanced up at the evening sky and winced at the unveiling of its moon. If I stayed much longer, I would be in danger of climbing a treacherous trail in the dark. I couldn't waste time contemplating my unexplained madness. I needed to leave now.

A warm towel was placed across my shoulders.

I gasped and spun around.

"Excuse me, miss. I didn't mean to startle you. But you looked like you needed to borrow my towel."

I looked up and squinted at the tall figure that hovered above my head. He stood there for an awkward moment before clearing his throat and kneeling by my side. I bristled in fear and tried to slide away, but I was only able to move a few inches.

"Oh, please don't be afraid. I'm not trying to hurt you. I thought you may have been in trouble. I noticed you were pretty close to the water, and your clothes were wet and covered with sand. I was afraid you drowned."

My eyes met his face, and my breath caught in my throat.

A glorious man sat before me.

He ran his hand through his dark brown hair and smiled. His steel gray eyes were large and commanding and were framed by two high cheekbones. His body was lean, yet muscular, visibly sculpted under a tight white t-shirt. He stretched his long legs out in front of himself and crossed his feet. I looked away with a twinge of embarrassment. I was staring.

"Do you usually prefer to swim in your clothes?" He eyed me curiously. His smile widened to a flash of perfectly white teeth. My gaze wandered back to his eyes and froze. They were subtly changing in color from chrome to black. I all at once became tongue-tied.

"I . . . I wasn't . . . trying to swim. I found myself walking too close to the water, and I fell in." My face stung with mortification. I quickly tried to wipe away the sand that had dried on one cheek. He respectfully looked away at the sight of my unease.

"Wow. That same thing happened to me one time. I came out here to do a little thinking, and I wasn't watching where I was going. My foot got caught in a hole, and I fell face-first into the water. I was thankful no one was there to see it happen. Not very many people visit this part of the beach. Do you come here often?"

I blinked and forced myself to break free from his mesmerizing visage. I had to find something to distract my eyes from wandering back. Something. A shell, his footprint, a log—anything. I focused on a small rock and studied it intently.

"No. I don't come here often."

"What brings you here then?"

Out of the corner of my eye, I could see his eyes were searching for mine. I tried to slow my heart which was rapidly picking up speed. I didn't want him to notice the thumping pulse that bulged in my neck.

"I was taking a drive and lost track of where I was going. I thought it would be nice to take a walk by the beach. I guess I came here to think, too."

His hand combed through his slicked-back hair, causing several pieces to cascade in front of his furrowed brow. There was a long pause as if he considered asking his next question.

"What were you thinking about?" he whispered.

I turned back to face him, and his eyes locked with mine. My hand searched for a fistful of sand, and I squeezed it. Several sharp grains found their way behind the thin band of gold that circled my left finger. I swallowed the lump that formed in my throat and quickly looked away. I haven't even thought about Ryan once. Here I sat, enamored with a perfect stranger, never once remembering the faithful fiancé who waited for me at home. I suddenly became disappointed in my fickle emotions. I allowed for a nameless man to captivate me in a way that only Ryan should.

"I'm very sorry. How rude of me not to introduce myself sooner. My name is Marcus," he said, interrupting my thoughts. His full lips curved into a smile as he extended his hand for mine. It suspended in the air briefly while I contemplated touching it.

"My name is Gwendolyn," I managed to say. I touched the warm skin of his hand and let out a sharp cry. The veil that covered the eyes of my heart had been torn away, and I was able to see every hidden thing. I saw my marriage. I saw my children. I saw my life old and full of years.

I saw it all with him.

I recoiled my hand in confusion and quickly stood to my feet. A final glimpse of the setting sun had disappeared behind him, creating a shadow that threatened to rob my trail's visibility. My awareness quickly returned, and my sensibility kicked into gear. I didn't have time to entertain awkward conversations with charismatic strangers. My parents were probably wondering where I was. I looked down at my soiled clothes and brushed off the sand.

"Thank you for your towel. That was very thoughtful of you. But I really must be on my way." I made as little eye contact as possible. I pulled the towel from my shoulders and handed it to him.

"You're welcome. I'm just glad I was able to help. Are you leaving so soon?" His long, muscular legs swept him up in one graceful motion. He lightly brushed off the sand that clung to his khaki cargo shorts.

"I am. I need to get back to my car before it gets too dark. I'm parked over there." I pointed to the top of the cliff. He looked up in the direction of my finger and frowned.

"But that's at the top of the mountain. Do you know your way through the trail?"

"I do," I lied, purposing to avert my eyes.

I abruptly turned around and started walking to its entrance. I was hoping he wasn't paying attention to our conversation when I mentioned I hadn't visited this part of the beach.

"Are you sure?" he asked, falling in step behind me. "I know the trail well. It's overgrown with bushes and trees. There's a lot you can trip over if your daylight is missing. And the cliff's edge is pretty abrupt. One misstep could—" His voice broke. "One misstep could be fatal. I would feel awful if something happened to you, and I could've prevented it. Can I walk you back to your car?"

I stopped in my brisk walk and spun around to face him. His posture straightened when his worried eyes met mine.

Yes. There was no doubt about it. He was as attractive as he was mysterious. His considerate gestures were something of a rarity in a day when people couldn't care less for their fellow man. But I didn't know who this person was. A faint voice in the back of my head told me that a hiking trail winding through a dark mountainside was the perfect place for a masher to make his move.

"I'm very thankful for your kindness. I really am. But I think I'll be okay on my own. It was nice meeting you today, Marcus." I turned back around. I quickened my pace as I approached the mountain.

"You don't trust me, do you?" His voice sounded offended.

I stopped and turned at his statement.

"You don't trust me, and that's okay. I wouldn't trust me either if I were you." He chuckled and took a few steps forward. "And I know this looks bad. I'm a guy, and you're a girl. It's late, and we're all alone. Common sense tells you not to trust this situation. But you don't know me. I don't have any other motive than to make sure you make it back to your car in one piece. I promise you this, I'm not trying to hurt you. If it makes you feel any safer, I can follow ten steps behind you. You won't even know I'm there. I'll just be able to go to bed tonight knowing you're safe in your car and not hanging off of that." He pointed to a large rock that descended below the parking lot.

He had made a valid point. If the trail was difficult to maneuver in the day, I knew it would be twice as challenging in the dark. What made my predicament worse was that no one knew where to find me if I went missing. I would become just another unfortunate statistic.

I would become just like Emma.

The gamble now was to choose between the lesser of the two evils. I sought out his face that was almost completely hidden in the night's spreading darkness. All of his features were blurred from my vision. All except one. His eyes were genuine.

"Okay. I guess you can follow me from a distance. I don't know what else to say other than thank you for caring.

Please understand, I'm not trying to be rude. I just don't know who you are."

"I'm honored I can help." He nodded his head in a bow. His expression became serious when he looked into my face. "It was a pleasure meeting you today, Gwendolyn."

"Nice to meet you, too, Marcus."

I turned back around and entered the pathway that climbed in the darkness.

The hike was painfully difficult. Broken tree branches and craggy rocks grabbed at my legs every step I took. Even though I was careful not to rush through the trail, I was constantly aware of Marcus's presence, which gave me a sense of urgency. The snapping of branches and the crushing leaves faintly echoed mine. When I stopped, he stopped. When I progressed, he progressed. He was respectful to his word, staying completely out of sight.

Ten steps apart.

As I turned the corner of the trail, my foot hooked under a knotted root of a tree, and I fell face-first to the ground. I bit the inside of my cheek to keep from screaming. An explosion of pain shot up my left knee. I didn't need a flashlight to see the gravel tore into my flesh.

"Gwendolyn? Are you okay?" His voice sounded troubled. I listened for his approach, but he remained still.

"Yes, I'm all right. I just tripped over a root and scraped my knee a little bit. Thank you." I inspected it under the dim light of the moon. A large streak of blood was already seeping through my torn jeans. I slowly stretched my leg and moaned. My movement was agonizingly restricted, but my leg wasn't broken. I took in a deep breath and hoisted my body to a stand. My knee buckled under the weight of pressure, and I stumbled forward with a scattering of rocks.

"Are you sure you're all right?" the worried voice asked again. A slight rustle of leaves sounded from his direction and then stopped.

"Yeah, I'm fine. I just lost my footing for a second there. Thanks, Marcus."

I licked the sweat that collected on my lips and swallowed. I needed to finish this. My leg hurt badly, and I knew I was dealing with more than a scrape, but I wanted nothing more than to be sitting in my car, driving home. I summoned all the remaining strength I had left and pushed my unwilling body up.

Every step I took was excruciatingly difficult. Just when I felt I could take no more, the hazy lights of the highway peeked through the top of the trail. I forced myself over the rocky ledge and hobbled into the dimly lit turnout. I could tell my knee was beginning to swell as my pant leg had become uncomfortably tight.

I bent at my waist and struggled to catch my breath. As I stood gasping for air, I strained to listen for Marcus's movement. There was none. The only sound I heard was the soft chirping of crickets and the faint crashing of surf. I glanced over the cliff and looked down into the dark, plunging trail. Somewhere within a tangled mess of trees and rocks, Marcus stood silently waiting for my car to start. He had been honest about his intentions from the start.

He kept his promise.

"Good night, Marcus," I whispered.

Chapter Four

Everywhere I looked, he was there. When I awoke, he was there. When I slept, he was there. When I looked in the mirror, when I took a shower, when I got dressed in the morning, he was there. There wasn't a day that went by that I didn't feel his metal eyes burning into mine. Two weeks ago, I left Marcus at the edge of the cliff, but he never left my side. The harder I fought to keep out his presence, the harder he fought his way back in.

And I fought hard.

The guilt of thinking of someone other than Ryan was unbearable. And I didn't know for sure, but something in me told me he sensed something was wrong. He was becoming more and more reserved as an already-taxed relationship had an even greater divide. Our conversations had become shallow and lacked substance, consisting of topics like changes in weather and new television shows to watch. All talk of marriage had ceased. Secrets began to fill a relationship that prided itself on honesty. Perhaps I should have told him about the night I went to the beach. At first, it seemed only sensible to lie. I didn't want to worry him with my careless decisions, and at the end of the day, my lesson had been learned. I rationalized away any guilt of dishonesty by reminding myself that I committed no wrong. Still, our communication never felt the same. I was at a loss for truth when he questioned my black-and-blue knee. I told him I slammed it on a step while falling down my stairs. I could still picture his face as he eyed me in disbelief. I was a bad liar, and he knew it. But the strange thing was, he never pressured me for the real story. Maybe he just didn't care. And so, the deterioration of our relationship slowly began to take place.

I looked down at my ring and studied the white flecks of light that were imprisoned in the small stone. An image of Marcus's smile surfaced, and I reached to grab my phone. I pressed the dial button for the third time and slowly paced the floor.

"Hey! It's me, Ryan. I'm not here to answer your call right now, but my machine is. Later."

"Ryan, it's me. I don't know why you're not answering your phone. This is the third time I've tried calling you. Anyways, I just wanted to tell you I'm running a little late. Maybe twenty minutes or so. Call me when you get this message. Okay? Love you."

I ended the call with a pang of disappointment and looked into my dresser mirror. As I quickly put on a swipe of lip gloss, I tried to think positively. Ryan never ignored my calls. His phone was probably on vibrate, and he didn't feel it ringing. Or maybe he was in an out-of-service area and didn't know I called. Whatever it was, I knew I had nothing to fear because he had nothing to hide. I couldn't project my shaky fidelity on his side of the relationship.

I finished my makeup with a heavy coat of eyeliner and sat back from my reflection. Despite my careful application of concealer and sparkly eye shadow, my eyes still looked desperate for a good night's sleep. I grabbed my purse and a pair of sunglasses and headed for the door.

***

Ryan pushed the basket of onion rings to the center of the table and leaned back in his chair. "I'm all finished with these. Do you want any?"

I looked down at my half-eaten chicken sandwich and struggled to swallow a mouthful of fries. It felt like I was trying to swallow cotton. The thought of finishing my lunch made my stomach twist in knots. "No thanks. I think I'm finished, too."

"What's wrong with your food? You weren't hungry today or something?" He glanced down at my plate and sneered. He picked up his cup of soda and took off the lid to eat the ice.

My hands balled in my lap as I watched a server deliver another table's order. How do I tell him that a simple date at a restaurant has become unbearably awkward? The conversation between us was worse than pulling teeth.

How did it get this bad?

"I don't know why I'm not hungry. I guess my eyes were bigger than my stomach. I should've just ordered a side of zucchini wedges."

"Well, are you ready to leave then? I don't want to hang around here all day. Their air conditioner must be broken or something because it's hot in here."

Without further discussion, he stood to his feet and threw the remains of his onion rings in the trash. He walked to the front counter to get my food bagged and handed me the sack.

He used to carry it for me!

He exited the restaurant without looking back, leaving me to trail behind him.

"So, where do you want to go now?" he asked, sounding impatient.

Several pretty girls wearing bikinis crossed our path to get into a car. I turned my head in the opposite direction and focused on a tree. I couldn't bear the thought of him checking them out.

"Uh, I don't know. Where would you like to go? The beach?" I suggested weakly.

"No. I'm tired of going to the beach. Let's see what's going on over there." He pointed to a group of people walking around a farmer's market.

"Oh, a farmer's market. Okay, that sounds great."

"Okay. Let's go then."

I stretched out my hand in expectation for him to grasp it, but he didn't. He thrust his hands into his pockets and started walking in the direction of the crowd. Although the sidewalk was alive with Saturday's excitement, we walked together in complete silence. I watched as several couples walked past, hands intertwined, lost in conversation. A pang of envy pierced me like a knife as I remembered sharing the same compatibility with him only weeks earlier. I glanced at his face and became discouraged by an unexpected expression. He was repulsed.

His pace quickened to a stride as he approached a table selling handmade soap. I joined the pressing customers and pretended to look at a bottle of hand lotion.

"Ryan?"

"Yeah?"

"Ryan, we need to talk."

"What about?" he muttered, not looking up from smelling a stick of incense.

"We need to talk in private. Can we go somewhere else?" I reached for his hand, but he pulled away.

"Why? What do we need to talk about that can't be discussed here?"

"I want to talk about us. But I'd rather do it in private."

"Why? What is there to say? You're so involved in your own little world, and now you want to take notice of mine?"

I sputtered to say something in response, but he walked to a table selling hemp necklaces.

"Ryan, please. It's really uncomfortable discussing our relationship in front of all these people. Can we please go somewhere else? I don't care where . . . that fountain over there has a few picnic benches. Or a parking lot? Just somewhere else?" The sandwich I had eaten earlier threatened to resurface.

He put down the bracelet he was holding and spun around to face me. "What do you want to talk about? You're different. You've been different ever since Emma went missing. And I'm not talking about you grieving over your best friend. I can understand all that. You're so different, it's like you've been living on another planet. I talk to you, and you don't seem to listen. No, I think the word is care. You don't seem to care. You don't ask me how my day went. You don't tell me about yours. You don't even show me affection anymore. Do you know how many times this month you wanted to talk about our wedding?" He held up his hand and made a zero. "Zero times."

"But—"

"Zero times!"

An old lady standing in front of us turned around at the change in his voice.

"What does that mean for our relationship? Huh? What does that mean?"

"I don't . . ."

"What does that mean?!" He picked up my left hand and pinched my ring. "What does this mean?" His eyes narrowed on mine before dropping my hand in disgust. He turned his back at the sight of my distraught expression and walked a few feet from where I stood.

I took a few steps toward him and stopped. "Ryan, please. You're embarrassing me. Can we please go somewhere else?" My eyes filled, and I blinked, sending two hot tears streaming down my cheeks.

"It's okay, Gwendolyn."

I looked across the crowded marketplace. Marcus was watching me.

"You want to go somewhere else and talk? Fine. We can go somewhere else and talk," Ryan turned from the table of necklaces and walked away.

"It's going to be okay. I'm here for you," Marcus's voice whispered in my head.

"What's up? Do you want to go or what?" Ryan asked, turning back around. He noticed my perplexed stare and strained to look in the same direction. "What's wrong with you? You look like you just saw a ghost."

A large group of tourists blocked my view of Marcus. When they cleared, he was gone. I turned back to Ryan and wiped my wet cheeks. "Okay," I muttered. "Let's go talk."

***

I stood at the back of the church and frantically smoothed the satin ruffles that gathered at my waist. I was excited, and it took a conscious effort to keep myself from fidgeting. I wiped my sweaty palms down the sides of my dress and began to pace in a small circle. My dad joined me from a hallway nearby and kissed me on my cheek.

"You look so happy, my darling," he whispered, straightening the veil that draped across my face. He looked at my bouquet of orchids for a thoughtful moment before handing them to me. I took the fragrant bundle into both hands and held it tightly against my chest.

"That's because I am. I've waited for this day for so long, and now it's finally here!" I was barely able to keep my voice from yelling.

The organ music played softly, signaling for the flower girl and ring bearer to step forward. The double doors opened slowly, and they disappeared into the sanctuary. The butterflies in my stomach fluttered with anticipation.

"Have I told you how proud I am of you? You're going to make such a good wife and mother someday."

I turned to my father and gave him a sideways glance. "Whoa, Dad. Not so fast. Let me get married first, and then we can talk about kids." I grimaced at the thought, and he chuckled at my expression.

"Oh, you know how aspiring grandparents can be. We just can't wait to hear the pitter-patter of little feet running through our houses." He tightened the knot of his silver necktie and hooked his arm around mine. He smiled and gave it a pat. "But, seriously. Make sure you guys get to work on that as soon as you can." His eyes crinkled as he tried to suppress the laughter that was building.

"Come on, that's gross! Dads aren't supposed to talk about stuff like that. Now I think I'm really going to throw up."

We both started laughing, and the double doors opened to a dramatic tone. All amusement washed from my face as I straightened my posture to enter.

"Here we go," I whispered.

"Here we go, sweetheart."

The muscle in my father's arm tightened when we stepped out of the inner room and into the main sanctuary. Both sides of the church stood up as we walked down the center aisle that seemed to stretch for miles. From the corner of my eye, I caught a glimpse of my mother wiping her eyes with a tissue.

I took a deep breath and stopped before a pastor who was positioned behind a small, stone pulpit. The music faded to a hum, and his attention shifted to my father.

"Who gives away this woman to be married?"

My dad unhooked his arm from mine and cleared his throat. "I do."

"Thank you. You may be seated."

My father turned around and winked before joining my family in a pew nearby.

I turned to my side and faced Marcus, who took both of my hands in his. His gray eyes darkened as he studied my every feature.

"You look beautiful, my wife."

My eyes opened, and I woke up.

"Marcus," I whispered.

Chapter Five

I checked the time on my cell phone and squinted back to the vacant parking lot. My eyes searched for any sign of a white truck before concentrating on the shoreline in front of me.

Ryan was late—forty-seven minutes late. It was becoming a common occurrence for him to suddenly lose track of time. Twenty minutes late here. Forty minutes late there. All with vague explanations of why. His attitude was always nonchalant, matter-of-fact, and at times indifferent. If I expressed any frustration with his unusual behavior, he would respond with defense and flip the blame to me. I was unjust for condemning him as he was only stopping by Joey's house or filling his tank with gas. At times, I was left wondering if I was justified in feeling upset. I hoped today would hold some measure of importance to him. But it didn't.

I let out a disappointed sigh and pressed the dial button on my phone. His voicemail picked up after only ringing once.

"Ryan, it's me. Where are you? I've been sitting here for at least forty-five minutes staring at an empty parking lot. You did say to meet you at three, right? Well, I don't know. If you don't show up soon, I'm just going to leave. Call me when you get this message."

I closed my cell phone with a snap and threw it. How could he do this to me today? Didn't he care that it was my birthday? What could possibly be more important to him than this? I shook my head in disgust and buried my feet deeper in the sand. I knew better than to ponder such matters. Ryan had become just as much of an enigma as anything else in my life. To try and figure him out was like being trapped in quicksand—it got me nowhere. My eyes wandered to lifeguard station twelve, where he knelt on one knee and proposed. How radically my life changed since that starry night on the beach. In just a few short weeks, I lost all I held dear to my heart—my best friend who had been missing for more than a month, and my fiancé who appeared to be having second thoughts.

I glanced at the parking lot that remained empty and quickly stood to my feet. He wasn't coming, and I wasn't going to sit around all day and wait for him to show up. I brushed away the sand from the back of my jeans and purposed to walk in the opposite direction of the lot. I held my head high as a painful reality set in. I needed to consider other options for my future, and perhaps Ryan wasn't one of them. I hastily pried the ring from my left finger and slipped it into my pocket. The decision had become quite clear. If I strived to obtain a relationship with someone, I would inevitably strive to maintain it. I didn't want to force something that should be there naturally. And I wasn't looking to pry open doors that were clearly bolted shut. I resisted the temptation to return to my car and deliberated the future before me.

My toes pressed deep in the wet sand as I followed the foaming line of surf that extended along the shore. I watched the water roll in and recede, leaving a wake of scampering sand crabs and fragmented shells in its path. I picked up a halved mussel and studied its pearly blue center before throwing it back to the ground. A large group of seagulls circling nearby landed to investigate the object that was discarded. I watched them fight over the trivial offering as contempt slowly invaded my heart.

Why?

Why would he stand me up on my birthday? Why would he choose a day like today to be so careless with his punctuality? Was his blatant disregard for our relationship a sign that he was cheating? Was there someone else who demanded for his attention more than me? It would explain his emotional withdrawal. The hostile defense to my probing questions suddenly made sense. But why plan for a date at the beach if there wasn't any intention to follow it through? It would've been easier for him to pretend to be sick than to deal with the messy aftermath of broken plans. Why not avoid the whole situation altogether?

If he would only tell me the truth about things!

If I knew the real story, I could separate fact from fiction and move on with my life. Yes, I would be crushed to lose him, and the thought of him loving someone else made my stomach twist in knots, but I needed to know.

The seagulls gave up their foolish squabble and began to follow my path for another handout. I glanced at the parking lot that held no promise and let out a sigh of defeat.

There was a slight possibility I had it all wrong. Perhaps Ryan grappled with his own suspicions he was choosing not to share. His detachment could be a deliberate form of protection. Our relationship had deteriorated to a fragment of its entity. He knew it was changing. I knew it was changing. As the morphing continued, we silently embraced the obscure while refusing to acknowledge its presence or the pain it produced. Our communication remained as it was—flawed.

My thoughts were interrupted by a massive wave that thundered behind me. I looked down at my feet and gasped as a flood of water rose above my ankles. I quickly bent over to roll up my jeans when another wave came spilling over the first. The tide had begun to rise. I stood to my feet and contemplated the white-capped waves that collided in the distance. Within a moment, the stretch of sand that was dry enough to walk on would be completely covered with water. The meditation on my failed relationship needed to continue somewhere else.

I turned on my heel to return to my car when a grouping of rocks grabbed for my attention. I squinted and considered the crescent formation that erected like a beacon in the shining sun. There was something about the location that struck an unexplored chord. Something that reminded me of Emma . . .

Emma?

It all came flooding back. She mentioned meeting her significant other at the tide pools after our argument. It never occurred to me that this part of the beach I visited so many times was probably where she spoke of. I looked around for any other site that matched her description. It was the only formation of rocks within walking distance of the party.

I thrust my hands deep into my pockets and walked in the direction that once called my best friend. At first, I didn't know what I was expecting to find. Emma's disappearance was never resolved, and in a bizarre way, I felt a type of closure just knowing she was once there. I drew close to the algae-covered rocks and ran my hand over its craggy exterior.

This was where she met him.

The one. Her soulmate. The man who knew her for a night and declared his devotion with a pearl necklace. All of her dreams of finding true love had finally come true. Or had it?

I could picture her sitting at the top of the rocks, looking at an ocean with problems too numerous to count. And what was the monster in her mind? Her missed chance to attend prom? Her lack of a boyfriend? Her best friend, who had it all? I bit my lower lip and swallowed the lump that formed in my throat. Her quest for happiness had become such a futile pursuit. She strived so hard to grasp the tiger by the tail, but the tiger turned around and gave her a fatal blow.

I suppressed the emotions that threatened to surface and climbed the rocks that towered above my head. A fine mist of saltwater sprayed against my face while the steady flow of waves crashed at my side. There was no question why Emma came here to think. All seemed right if given the proper vantage point.

After a few minutes of taking in the ocean's beautiful splendor, I searched the rock's surface for anything interesting to investigate. I carefully crossed the slippery exterior and peered into each hollowed-out mound. Greenish-gray limpets and bright purple sea urchins crowded every surface they could find. An orange-speckled sea star fought for its space amongst the imposing occupants. I reached for a sea anemone's tentacle and giggled when it clung to my outstretched finger. The view was lovely. It was as if I pulled up the ocean's blanket of waves, and I was able to catch a glimpse of the vast beauty that lay underneath.

I quickly stood to my feet and reached into my back pocket to grab my cell phone. If there was anything I could take home from my failed birthday at the beach, it would be a gorgeous picture for my corkboard. After checking each pocket with no success, I pulled my hand from my jeans and slowly lowered it to my side. I didn't have my phone. I threw it in anger after I hung up on Ryan's voicemail, and it was lying on the shore where I sat. I squinted back to the lifeguard station twelve and frowned at the growing predicament. I lingered longer than I had planned. The water rose considerably since I left, leaving the area awash with water and foam. If I hurried, I had a slight possibility of retrieving it before the tide covered the area completely.

But I had to leave now.

With my challenge clearly before me, I pulled my hair into a tight ponytail and strategized my steps through the accumulating puddles and seaweed. The surf at my back grew louder, forcing my carefully measured steps to become frantic. I suddenly wished I had worn different shoes. The soles of my ballet flats offered no traction for support. I shrieked as I stepped on a slick patch of algae, gliding my foot across the rock like a skateboard on cement. I stopped to stabilize my balance and cautiously continued with several steps forward.

The booming behind me intensified, delivering a flood of water that spewed across my path. I turned around and faced the ocean that commanded for my attention.

I had waited too long to leave.

My heart filled with unspeakable horror. The once-passive waves heaped into massive torrents and started hurling themselves where I stood. An enormous wave more powerful than the previous thundered hard against the rock. I gasped for air as a frigid blast of water sprayed across my face, temporarily blinding my vision to continue. I fell to my knees and wheezed while frantically groping for the rock to stabilize. Another wave ripped across the top, shooting a surge of water under my feet and knocking me to my side. A shoe slipped off my foot and danced across the rock before disappearing over the edge. With shaky hands, I fumbled to take my other shoe off and rolled to my stomach. My arms and legs clung to the rock in a death grip as an explosion of water rained from above.

Oh, God! Please help me!

I shut my eyes tight as another wave struck hard, sending my body reeling from the intense blow.

I fell backward and lost total control.

A loud cracking sounded. The back of my head struck the side of the rock, and I was tossed face-first into the ocean. For a horrifying moment, my vision was blurred while the wave sucked me deep into its powerful trenches. My body mercilessly tumbled like a ragdoll as bits of sand and shell shredded my skin like glass. My legs and arms thrashed wildly about. I opened my eyes through the burning salt and grit and located the ocean's floor with both feet. With one mighty kick, I pushed hard against the shifting bottom and propelled my body upward. The wave pulled back its relentless swing, and I writhed my way to the top.

My mouth gasped wildly for air, but a rush of water choked out my attempt. I gagged and sputtered as the salty liquid poured down the back of my throat. I fought hard to take another breath, but my effort was unsuccessful. A great fist of pressure suddenly seized my burning lungs while they begged for something they couldn't receive. My vision went gray as my oxygen-deprived body began to pass out, and my fighting ceased to continue. Another wave crashed above my head, sending my unmoving body spiraling under the water.

For one singular moment in time, my life flashed before my eyes as a picture book of memories flipped within my mind. I felt my mother's embrace, soft and fragrant, as she bandaged a scraped knee. My father's mustache tickled my cheek as he kissed me goodnight. My first dance at junior high, nervous and clumsy. Ryan knelt before the ocean, asking for my hand in marriage.

And then . . . darkness.

All memories faded to black, and an empty void sucked me into nothing.

A powerful force suddenly ripped me from my descent and pulled me to the surface. The two strong arms held my body high and, with one forceful push, squeezed the center of my stomach upward. I threw up the contents that engulfed my midsection and gasped wildly for air.

"Hold on to me tight!" the voice yelled over the thundering ocean.

Dazed, my arms obediently gripped around the wide, muscular back as we pitched high upon a wave. The water mounted to a staggering climax and fell with a crash, striking us both beneath its surface. My face tucked into the crook of his neck while his powerful arms fought quickly to pull us to the top. I sputtered out another mouthful of water and frantically gasped for air.

"Breathe!" the voice commanded.

My eyes widened in terror as my vision suddenly returned, and I realized how dangerously close to the rocks we were traveling. Another wave crashed above us, pounding us harder under its twisting current. His body wrapped around me like a tight cocoon. We descended further toward the ocean's floor. My leg pulled away from his waist and brushed against the rocky wall that threatened at my side.

Another wave will throw us into the rocks!

"You'll be okay, Gwendolyn. Trust me."

His body worked to get us to the surface, and I sputtered for more air. For a brief second, I was able to pull myself from his shoulder to look into his face.

"Breathe!" Marcus yelled.

I filled my lungs with air as the water began to mount. His body clung around me tightly while the wave peaked high and launched us straight into the rocks. Marcus screamed in pain as his back was pushed into the serrated edges, tearing into his flesh. I shut my eyes in terror. The wave pulled us back from the toothed wall and plunged us deeper into the water. His injured body struggled to pull us through the ocean's current, and we surfaced to the top.

"Breathe!"

His body stiffened in anticipation while the wave swung us back and punched us harder into the rocks. An agonizing cry sounded in my ears.

"You'll get through this. You're safe with me."

I opened my burning eyes and looked down at the splitting back that was selflessly shielding mine. Beneath the bloody sinews of shredded flesh and muscle, greenish-gray scales glimmered like glass in the setting sun. His arms hugged me tighter as my body slumped forward, and I fainted from shock.

I opened my eyes and silently watched from below. Marcus wildly stripped off his bloody t-shirt and pulled a hooded sweatshirt from the front seat of his car. His face grimaced in pain as he stretched the material across his mangled flesh that twisted from my sight. He knelt down, and with a gentle reverence, carefully picked up my unmoving body. He slid me into the backseat of his car and groaned. The black leather felt cool against my cheek that burned to the touch.

"Please hold on for me, Gwendolyn. Please . . ."

I closed my eyes and allowed for the deep hum of his engine to lull me to sleep.

The last thing I remembered hearing was his worried voice in my head, begging for me to hold on.

Chapter Six

There was beeping. A few hushed voices. The running of water in a sink. Latex gloves being fitted, followed by the soft rustle of plastic tearing. I opened my eyes to thin slits and looked around the dimly lit room. A nurse worked silently at my bedside as she hung a new bag of fluids and connected them to an IV. She pressed a few buttons on a beeping machine and scuffled to a nearby sink to wash her hands. Her face became pensive as she looked at her watch and scribbled something informative on a clipboard. She set the clipboard aside and walked to a large window, where she pulled the blinds closed even tighter. To my left, there was a nightstand with a bouquet of roses and balloons. To my right, there was a chair with my mother's purse draped across the top.

Her distant voice suddenly rose from the doorway. She paced around a thin man wearing a white lab coat and glasses.

His hands waved in elaborate gestures while she anxiously asked him for answers. After a few minutes of tense conversing, her posture slumped forward, and she began to sob. He motioned for her to follow him down the hall, and they disappeared from view.

I swallowed the painful lump that was lodged within my throat and grimaced. I needed water desperately. My mouth was so dry, I could feel it sucking moisture from deep within my chest. My hands fumbled for the sides of my bed in an attempt to prop myself up. An excruciating pain shot from the back of my head and traveled down to the lower end of my spine. I fell back to my pillow with an agonizing gasp.

"Water, please," my raspy voice croaked. My throat unexpectedly burned as a team of impaired muscles were exercised in speaking.

The tiny nurse who was opening the door to leave spun around to face me. "Gwendolyn, you're up? I wasn't expecting to see you awake so soon." She hurried to my bedside and knelt to hold my hand. Her wide eyes studied my face in pity. Perhaps she saw something I was unaware of. "Let me introduce myself. My name is Natalie. I'll be your nurse for today. Sure, I'll bring you some water. Maybe with a straw? How are you feeling?"

I licked my lips that cracked when I smiled and slowly shook my head. I dare not try to speak again.

"Not too good, huh? Okay, we can fix that. I'll let the doctor know you're awake, and he can give you something for the pain. And if you need anything else, please don't hesitate to ask. There's a button here on the side of your bed that will call me at the nurses' station. Just press intercom eight." She showed me a handheld paddle lined with different colored buttons and a remote control that operated my television. After noting where the restroom was located, she smoothed my arm and asked, "Are you comfortable in that position? I can move your bed up or down if you'd like."

I shook my head.

"Okay, then. I'll go get that water you asked for." She reached across my bed to turn on a lamp and slipped outside the door.

I carefully flipped my body to one side and moaned. It felt as though my limbs had been ripped off and put back together wrong. There was a deep ache within my bones that made moving unthinkable. The skin on my face burned like I scrubbed it on asphalt, and every time I swallowed, a mouthful of splinters ran down the back of my throat. I looked at the IV that was threaded in my arm and closed my eyes in discouragement.

I shouldn't be here.

I should be strewn across the ocean's floor. It was an absolute miracle I made it through that accident alive. I remembered my body giving up when I couldn't get enough air. My vision went black, and I could feel death take over.

I should be dead.

An image of Marcus pitching high upon a wave suddenly flashed through my mind. His agonizing screams rang loudly in my ears while his back was thrust repeatedly into a wall of jagged rocks.

Marcus.

He risked his life for mine and undoubtedly suffered for it. But why? Why would someone offer their life for a complete stranger? For someone who gave him the brush-off only weeks earlier? And his back . . .

What was in his back?

Why did I see fish scales in the place of flesh? It didn't make any sense. It wasn't his shirt. It wasn't a tattoo. It was the back of a fish under his torn skin. I must have been hallucinating at that moment. That would make sense. Perhaps it was the lack of oxygen to my brain or the hit to my head. My hand gingerly rose to the injury and felt a large, encircling bandage. I must have hit it harder than I thought.

"Hello, Gwendolyn. I'm Doctor Baker," the authoritative voice announced from the doorway. A tall doctor strode into the room with my mother and Natalie trailing in behind him. My mother's face flushed pink with grief when my puffy eyes met hers. She rushed to my side and rubbed my hand against her tear-stained cheek.

"Oh, my baby. My baby," she whimpered.

The nurse set a cup of water on my nightstand and took a few steps back. The doctor's voice broke through the quiet sobbing that permeated the room.

"Gwendolyn, I can offer you that water. But I'm afraid it won't go down easily. You're receiving a saline drip right now. Any dehydration you're feeling may just be local dryness in your mouth. I have sucrose lollipops to help with that." He pulled a chair close to my bed and studied my face intently. "I hear you're in a lot of pain."

I nodded.

"And I know it hurts to speak, so I'm not going to ask you any questions." He reached into his front pocket and pulled out a small pad of paper. "Natalie, will you run this prescription for me? Make it a twenty-milligram push . . . and a few sucrose lollipops. Gwendolyn, do you like orange or strawberry? Better bring both," he said with a wave of his hand. He scribbled something on the paper and handed it to the nurse. He then turned his attention back to me and pulled his stethoscope from around his neck. After doing a thorough vital check, he leaned back in his chair and exhaled deeply, obviously satisfied.

"Well, it looks like you're on the mend. Your vitals are great. Your CBC test came back normal. You're still slightly dehydrated, but we're working on that." He leaned over to check the saline drip. He adjusted the flow of the injection tube and sat back down. "Given your circumstances, you're the picture of perfect health. Now, I know yesterday may be a little foggy for you. So, let me bring you up to speed. You were brought into the hospital by a gentleman who said you were drowning in the ocean. You had a laceration to the back of your head about six inches long that required stitching. You also had some minor abrasions to your face that were probably caused from the friction of sand. And, more than likely, you drank a sufficient amount of saltwater because you were admitted delusional and dehydrated. Now, I'm going to anticipate you'll be sore for the next few days. Adrenaline will push your body to tread water past its limit. Which I'm sure it did. So, your muscles are taxed. And expect your throat to hurt from all that saltwater you swallowed. All things considered, I think you pulled out quite well. And if I were you, I would be thankful because it could've been a lot worse." He stood up from his chair and glanced at my mother, who was crumpled in the corner. "I was just mentioning to your mother that you must have a guardian angel watching over you because you were saved just in time."

Concern suddenly flooded my heart as Marcus came to mind. He took a larger beating than I did. Was he in the hospital, too?

"Marcus . . . what about Marcus?"

The doctor spun around, shocked that I spoke. "Marcus? Who's Marcus? Are you asking about the gentleman who brought you into the hospital?"

I nodded my head fervently.

"Well, from what I saw, he looked like he could've used some care. I suggested that he admit himself for an examination . . . at least for a quick vital check, but he refused. You can lead a horse to water, but you can't make him drink. He seemed considerably worried for you, though. And my guess is, if he was hurting that badly, he would've put some of that focus on himself. At any rate, I'll be in later tonight to check up on you. And I suggest you stay one more day for observation. You can be discharged first thing tomorrow morning." He eyed my disappointed expression and walked to the back of the room to wash his hands.

"Thank you, Dr. Baker," my mother's voice whispered.

"You're welcome. Just remember to call the front desk if you need anything. I'll be back in a few hours. Good night, ladies."

He looked at my chart one last time before nodding in dismissal and walking out the door.

My mother and I sat without speaking as the beeping of my heart monitor recorded my quickening pulse. I couldn't stop thinking about Marcus. I knew he needed medical help, yet he refused it when it was offered. Why? It pained me to know he was needlessly suffering from wounds he didn't deserve. I took the full weight of responsibility, knowing all of this could have been avoided if I had made wiser choices. It was so foolish of me to underestimate the tide. I should've left the beach after I discovered Ryan wasn't planning to show up. And Ryan . . .

What about Ryan?

I should be waking up to him pacing outside my hospital door, not my mother! I pushed my sheets to my waist and shifted my weight to one side.

My mother's chair suddenly squeaked loudly as she slid herself closer to my bed. She pulled another tissue from her purse and blew her stuffy nose.

"Oh, honey! How did this happen? I know it hurts to talk, so please don't say anything. But how? It was your birthday, and we had a nice celebration. You were excited about your date with Ryan and left the house to go meet him. And then, out of the middle of nowhere, I get a call from your cell phone from some strange man telling me he's taking you to the hospital. How did you wind up in the ocean, drowning? And what happened to your head?" She buried her face in her hands and heaved a loud sob. I attempted to answer her questions, but she stopped me with a wave. "Shh! No, honey. I don't need the answers from you now. I'm only venting. It just all seems so out of place. Ryan was going to do something special for you at the beach, right?"

I shrugged my shoulders.

"Well, where was he in all of this? I got a call from him at a quarter to six, telling me he couldn't find you. Yet, you mentioned to your father and me that you were planning to meet him at three o'clock. Where was he between three and six?"

I shrugged my shoulders again and shook my head. I had just as many questions as she did.

"I raced here as fast as I could. I see you battered in a hospital bed in the ICU. And all I can ask is why? Were you planning to swim yesterday without your bathing suit? And you're such a strong swimmer, honey. How did you let the ocean get you to a place of drowning?"

There was a knock at the door, followed by Natalie poking her head around the corner. Her bubbly countenance broke through the tension in the room. She walked to the foot of my bed and set down a handful of candy.

"Hi. It's me again. I have some medicine for you and those sucrose lollipops the doctor ordered. I was able to find strawberry, orange, and lemon. I hope they can help. Now, this medicine I'm going to give you may make you feel a little drowsy. So, just be forewarned. But it will help with your pain. And in a minute or two, you'll be feeling as right as rain." She unscrewed the IV and inserted the long tip of a syringe filled with narcotics. "You'll feel a slight burning sensation as I push it through your IV. Just tell me if I need to slow down, okay? Well, that's it. You may start to feel a little woozy now, and that's totally normal. Just don't fight the medicine to stay awake, or you'll get the jitters. Would you like me to lower your bed for you?"

I nodded my head, and she flattened my bed's position. The tight muscles in my neck relaxed while a warming sensation spread up my arm and traveled throughout my body.

All pain was slowly replaced with an overwhelming feeling of euphoria. I looked up at the nurse and gave her a lopsided grin.

"Thank you, Natalie," I said in a scratchy voice.

"You're very welcome! I'm just glad to finally see that pretty smile of yours. Call me if you need anything."

My vision began to gloss over, and my eyes drifted to my mother. She noticed my detached expression and gave a soft chuckle.

"It looks like you're starting to feel better."

"I am. I feel better than I have in a long time."

She rubbed my arm for a minute and walked to the window. "Well, don't worry about answering any of my questions tonight. What you need now is rest. Plenty of rest. We can talk about all the details when you feel better. I'm just glad you're alive."

I closed my heavy eyelids as the drug pulled me into a deeper tranquil state.

"Mom?"

"Yes, sweetheart?"

"Do you know where my clothes are that I wore yesterday?"

"Um . . . yes. I think they're here in a bag by the window. Yes, they're here. Why?"

"Can you look in the front pocket of my jeans for my engagement ring?"

"Your what?"

"My engagement ring."

"Your engagement ring?"

There was a crumpling of clothing as my mother fished it out of my pants.

"Yes, honey. Here it is. Would you like me to give it to you?"

"No," I whispered, allowing for sleep to take over. "Just hold on to it for me."

***

"Knock! Knock!" the eager voice announced from the hallway. My bedroom door creaked softly and opened to a crack. "Is it okay if I come in?"

I folded the magazine I was reading and set it on my nightstand. I glanced up at Ryan and nodded. He cleared his throat loudly and opened the door a bit wider.

"Yes, you can come in," I said, avoiding his looming form.

His long neck craned around my bedroom wall, and he stepped further into my room. I forced myself to give a phony smile that made me want to vomit. There was no joy in seeing him today. For the past two days, I had been on a roller-coaster of revelation and grief. He never visited me at the hospital. Although my stay was brief, I would have expected to see him at least once. Disappointment surfaced every time a nurse came through my door as I anticipated it to be him.

And the disappointment cut deep.

A simple phone call placed to my mother was not enough. I wanted to see the worried expression on his face. I wanted to feel his hand holding mine. I wanted him to be there! But he wasn't. The more I thought about Ryan's trespasses, the more repulsed I became. I felt myself falling out of love with someone who once held a singular place in my heart. He was egocentric and secretive. Or more properly put, a liar.

He kept his back hidden from sight while he carefully skirted around the foot of my bed and sat at my side. His smile became sheepish. He leaned forward and kissed the top of my head.

"I have something for you," he said, straightening his posture. He pulled his hand from around his back to reveal a plush white teddy bear. I tentatively accepted the presented gift and held it in my lap.

"Thank you," I said artificially. My eyes remained averted as I tugged on the doll's soft fur. Instead of our visit naturally transitioning into a carefree conversation, the room filled with unbearable silence. My eyes darted to his and then to the window.

"So, how is my love feeling today? Your head looks like it got a pretty bad lump." He reached forward and gently caressed the side of my temple.

Did he even know where I hit my head?

"It feels sore from time to time. But I think I'll be okay. I have a slash to the back of my head that's about six inches long. So, I guess the pain is to be expected." I looked at his face for any recognition and saw none.

"Oh, babe. That's awful. Six inches? Your mom told me you hit your head, but I didn't know you hit it that hard."

"And why is that? Why don't you know I hit my head hard?" I looked away in repulsion when his eyes became wide with confusion.

"Why don't I know you hit your head hard? Well, I don't know. Maybe because your mother didn't tell me all the details when I called? I would've preferred to talk to you, but she told me you were asleep and needed your rest. I didn't want to wake you."

"And was that the only time you could've called? Why didn't you try again later? Or better yet, why didn't you visit? There's nothing like seeing someone in person to understand a situation better. "

He shifted positions on my bed and looked at his fidgeting hands. "You're not mad about that, are you? Gwen, you were in the hospital for two days. And I wasn't even notified until the morning after the first. I would've made it a point to see you first thing, but I knew you needed your rest. Besides, isn't it better that we visit here in your room, where we can talk comfortably and not worry about nurses interrupting? Or, I don't know . . . your mother being there?" He looked at me and casually shrugged his shoulders, completely clueless about any wrongdoing.

I exhaled slowly and shook my head in irritation. "You don't understand, and I'm not sure why. When a loved one gets hurt and is in the hospital, it doesn't matter who's there or if it's comfortable for you or not. You just want to be there with them. I was lying in a bed with an IV up my arm, in an agonizing amount of pain. Do you think I was comfortable? Remember, this isn't all about you. You should want to be there because you are concerned for my well-being. You should want to be there because you love me." I was suddenly grateful for my severed emotions that wouldn't allow for tears.

"Babe, I'm sorry. I blew it. I didn't know I offended you that badly. I was under the impression that you were resting in the hospital and were coming home soon. I had no idea you would become so offended if I chose to visit you here. But if something matters to you, it matters to me. And for that, I'm sorry." He tried to tilt my chin to meet his gaze, but my focus remained fixed on the teddy bear in my lap.

"What about my birthday? That mattered to me. Did it matter to you?"

He stood at my question and quickly walked to my dresser. The wood groaned beneath the weight of his body as he leaned on its surface with both elbows. He took a long time to answer.

"Of course it mattered. Why do you think I was late?" His eyebrow arched high in a look of offense. His question hung in the air and lingered like a bad stink. After seeing I wasn't going to speak, he answered his own question, "I was late because I was buying you a birthday gift."

"Then why didn't you answer my calls?"

"Because I didn't want you to know I forgot to buy it! I had our date all planned out, but I didn't buy you a gift? How bad does that look? And what was I supposed to say when you called? Hey, babe, I'm here at the mall buying your birthday gift last minute? Come on! That would look so insensitive."

"But ignoring my numerous phone calls was any better? I waited for close to an hour for you! Why couldn't you lie and make up some excuse to let me know you were still coming? Something! Like I would've cared about the truth anyways?" I picked up the bear in my lap and tossed it across the room. He looked down at my empty hands and froze.

"Where's your ring?"

"I took it off."

"You took it off? Why?"

"Because I don't trust you anymore."

He pushed himself away from my dresser and walked to the foot of my bed. His alarmed face paled as he scanned my numb expression.

"Why don't you trust me?"

"Because you never are where you say you'll be. Your excuses are vague, maybe even lies for all I know. And you don't return any of my phone calls. It seems to me you have something to hide."

A sudden sheen of sweat gathered at his brow, and he wiped it. He stepped in a bit closer. "Why do you think I have something to hide?"

"Because you don't care. You have a disconnection from me that I can't understand. And quite frankly, I have one from you, too."

He spun around to walk back to my dresser and stopped. There was a lengthy pause in our argument while he fought to control his emotions. I didn't need to see his face to know he was crying.

"What can I do to prove to you that I still love you?" his voice whispered.

I thought about his question that presented no answer. "I don't know."

Chapter Seven

"Marcus," I whispered.

I sat up from the delusion that visited so often and stared into darkness. The sinking feeling of disappointment revisited while the familiar shadows of my bedroom slowly took their forms. Another night of blissful dreaming proved to be nothing more than fiction. And yet, I was always deceived into believing they were real. The church was packed with guests, too many at times to be seated in pews. My father would joke about having grand-children and would laugh when he saw my reaction to his humor. Marcus's voice would whisper lovingly in my head as I walked down the center aisle to join him. And his eyes—his penetrating eyes would change from metal to onyx as they burned deep into mine. I didn't want to wake up from my dreams anymore.

I wanted them to be real.

My body shivered from a gust of wind that broke through my parted curtains and whirled about my exposed flesh. Every so often, I could feel the ocean in the breeze that blew through my bedroom window. Tonight was one of those times. I closed my eyes and drank in the aromatic air that filled my heart and mind.

Go to the beach.

Unhesitatingly, I threw my legs over the side of the bed and searched for my shoes. My hands scrambled wildly in the darkness as I slipped on a pair of sandals and tied a fleece sweater around my waist. In my usual routine, I reached for my car keys and then stopped. There was no need to drive tonight. A trail that led to a private access to the beach could easily be entered through our backyard. It was a simple walk, and I knew it well. It was probably a better route to take anyways, as the start of my car would undoubtedly wake my parents. Although I was nineteen years old and old enough to make my own decisions, my father wouldn't approve of his daughter engaging in a spontaneous drive at midnight. He'd raise questions that required logical answers. Ones I didn't have.

The sudden contemplation of my parents conjured a brief sobriety of thinking. The rational part of my consciousness bantered with the determined. Suppose my father needed to use the restroom and decided to poke his head through my doorway? What if he discovered I was missing?

I walked to the foot of my bed and slowly took a seat. I wasn't planning to be gone for long, an hour or two at the most. The risk of something happening within that time frame was pretty hard to imagine. Still, I shouldn't take any chances.

I jumped to my feet and gasped as a blast of air knocked a picture frame off my dresser, and it landed on the floor with a crash.

If I were planning to leave, the time was now!

I reached for my clothes that were scattered across the floor and skillfully shaped them into my body's reclined form. I then tucked my comforter under the long, protruding hump and crept out the door.

I stepped out from my house's shadow and into the spreading night, where a strong breeze felt invigorating as it cooled my flushed skin. I tied back my hair that spun across my face and walked down the familiar grassy hill. I visited the trail just about every other day in the hot summer months. I'd run from my yard with a bodyboard in tow, hardly stopping to remove the stones that gathered in my sandals. Not only was it a passageway to the ocean's refreshing waves, but a place of refuge from life's frequent storms. I often found myself staring at grass and logs while I brooded over some new pestering problem. The past adorned the trail with melancholy and memory, but tonight it would serve a different purpose.

I jumped over rocks that were hidden in shadows and ducked under branches that were camouflaged from sight. My pace quickened to an excited sprint when the rumbling of waves grew louder. I took off my sandals that encumbered my feet and slung them over one shoulder. The prickle of grass transitioned to a silky stretch of sand. My eyes fell in first, drinking in the mesmerizing view.

Come to me.

As an unassuming moth is drawn to the irresistible flame, so my body was pulled closer toward the ocean. My gaze never wavered while bits of rock and fragmented shell pierced the tender soles of my feet. I stopped at the foaming break of waves and waited for the water to make its move. It touched the tops of my feet and beckoned for me to draw closer. Unquestioningly, I answered its alluring call and took another step. The water spilled across the sand and rose above my ankles.

Come closer.

I nodded my head in agreement and took another step. The waves mounted to foamy white peaks and crashed against the shore. A surge of water spread across the sand and rose to my shins. I looked down at my pants that were covered in sand and moved in its direction. The water laid a blanket of foam, and I responded without question. My heart hammered in my chest while I anticipated its command.

I waited . . .

. . .

Nothing. The connection I felt with the ocean around me had all at once vanished in a ripple of sweeping foam. I looked down at my arms that reached for the water and slowly lowered them to my sides.

Something wasn't right.

I was dressed in my pajamas, standing knee-deep in freezing water, and none of it made any sense. My decision to visit the beach was as frightening as it was bizarre. And I didn't know for sure, but something told me it happened in the past. For some reason, it was difficult to retrieve the exact details. I flinched as an icy wave splashed against my waist, and I ran back to the shore.

I studied the shadows that moved across the water while fragments of memories began to trickle in. I've had a peculiar attraction to the ocean I never could explain. I've walked out to the water and yearned for something more. I've done all of this before!

Or did I? Why did it feel so vague? Why was it blurry, like it happened in a dream or a thought? How could I forget so much? My eyes burned as my vacant stare distorted, and I blinked.

Why was I here?

What was I doing at the beach at such a ridiculous time of night? Why would I want to confuse things by coming out so late? Like I didn't have enough confusion in my life already? This was just what I needed! A midnight stroll to set off a year's worth of lecturing from my father. I could see my parents now: worried looks on their faces, nervously pacing the living room floor, checking the window every two minutes for my arrival.

I yanked the sweater from around my waist and slipped both sandals on my feet. My parents wouldn't understand my choice to sneak out of the house, no matter what excuse I gave. And how could I blame them? I didn't understand my choices myself!

I checked my pocket for my house keys and pulled my sweater over my head. If I hurried, I would be lucky enough to avoid any questioning from my parents altogether. I looked to the sea one last time before turning toward the hill to leave.

I turned around and ran into Marcus.

My face slammed hard against his chest, and I was unexpectedly thrown backwards. He lurched forward and extended his hand for help.

"Oh, Gwendolyn! Are you okay?" His hands firmly gripped both of mine and pulled me to a stand. I sprang forward and nervously brushed away the imaginary sand that covered my clothes. My tousled hair parted from my eyes, and I stopped in my anxious fidgeting. His metallic eyes burned with expectancy as they eagerly sought for mine. My stare finally united with his, and his lips slowly parted to a smile.

"Are you okay?" his smooth voice asked.

I shut my eyes and felt my face grow hot. "Yes, I am. Thank you. It looks like you're always there when I need help."

A strong gust of wind blew between us, parting his collared white shirt to reveal a perfectly sculpted body. His left pectoral muscle flexed tight in the moonlight. My inspection of his flawless visage broke as he uttered a deep chuckle and took a small step forward.

"How are you feeling? I've been so concerned about you." His expression suddenly darkened, and he reached forward to gently touch the back of my head. My nerve endings tingled when his warm hand softly connected with the surface of my skin. His ebony black eyes fastened to mine. I struggled to look away.

I couldn't.

"I wanted to visit you at the hospital," he breathed. "But I didn't know how you would take to seeing me. Your mother didn't know it, but I stood from afar and listened as she talked to a doctor about your condition. I couldn't leave the hospital until I knew you were going to be okay." He slowly lowered his hand from the back of my head and swallowed. My eyes fell from his and filled with hot tears.

He was probably standing there in pain while he listened for the outcome of my health. My wounds were being bandaged as his were left unattended. Was he really so concerned for my well-being that he would neglect to care for himself? And Ryan would dare to complain about a visit being uncomfortable because of a few interruptions from a nurse? Ha! This man has shown more consideration for me in the brief encounters we've had than Ryan has shown in our whole relationship put together! Such a self-sacrificing person took me by surprise.

"You shouldn't worry about wanting to see me. I would've loved a visit at that dreary, old hospital. You saved my life, and you didn't have to . . ." My voice fell as I fought to keep from crying. His warm eyes held me where his arms did not.

I took in a shaky breath and carefully chose the words I've yearned to say for days. "I'm very grateful for what you've done. I think about how close I came to dying, and it scares me. I wouldn't be standing here today if it weren't for your selflessness. I don't know if I would've done something like that for someone I didn't know. You could've gotten yourself killed. I feel awful that you got hurt because of my foolish decisions. I've thought about that day every day since it happened. And I wish I could take it all back. But I can't." I reluctantly continued at the sight of his discomfort. I frowned and whispered, "I've been worried for you, too. My doctor told me you refused to be seen even though he felt you needed medical care. And I know you were hurt pretty badly from what I saw—your back on the rocks, that is."

His face grimaced as if my comment pained him, and he broke eye contact. He suddenly became uncomfortable. His body shifted positions, and his attention diverted to the waves at his side. Something bobbed in the distance, and his eyes narrowed. "You said you would've taken back that day if you were given a chance. But I ask you, why? All things happen for a reason, right? We don't understand the details of our lives because we're so busy living day to day. We need to take a few steps back and take the whole picture in." He knelt to the ground and picked up a small hermit crab that scurried to his shoe. "I risked my life for you that day, and I would do it again. I don't have to know you're special to know you're worth dying for. Don't feel responsible for what happened to me out there. It was a choice I made willingly." He threw the crab toward the ocean and turned to study my face. "Your life is more important than mine."

I cocked my head to one side and felt myself frown. His comment struck me as odd. Humans' mentality was always skin for skin. It was deeply ingrained within our nature to pre-serve oneself, no matter what the cost. Most people wouldn't only run from death's calling but would trample over whoever got in the way to do so. He didn't even bat an eye to give his life for a complete stranger. And with no pretenses! He suffered for someone else's well-being without the need for tributes or honor. He wouldn't have even gotten a 'thank you' if we hadn't met by chance.

He dug his hands deep into his pockets and chuckled softly. "What I'm finding so intriguing is why you're here at such a late hour." His powerful eyes softened as they playfully inspected mine.

I couldn't help but smile and shrug my shoulders in bewilderment. There were no logical explanations as to why I was here. My mind quickly resorted to the answer I planned to give my parents. "I came here to do a little thinking. But what about you? Why are you here so late?" I anticipated he would notice my crafty attempt to shift the focus to him. But he didn't. He took the bait and ran with it.

"What am I doing here? Well, I just got off work. Sometimes I need to do a little thinking, too. And this place is just perfect for that kind of thing. I don't know . . . It's tranquil and quiet. It gives me a necessary break from the hustle of coworkers and customers." His muscular arm reached deep into his shirt as he scratched at a spot on his left shoulder blade. I resisted the temptation to stare at his exposed chest and looked at the sea behind him. For the first time, I noticed a silver necktie was tucked in the back pocket of his black-creased slacks.

"Where do you work? Someplace nice?"

"Yeah, I guess you can call it that. I don't know if you've heard of it before, but it's a club called La Mer. It just opened a few months ago."

"La Mer? Is that the place where The Silver Fox Steak House used to be? It's on GlenPoint Strip, right?"

"Yes. That's the one. It's the perfect place to hang out and have a good time. They have great music and even greater food. I could take you there sometime if you'd like." An unexpected timidity surfaced through his authoritative demeanor, and he crossed his arms against his flexed chest. His eyes pinned with interest while he waited for my response to his alluring proposal.

I gave him a weak smile as my smitten heart skipped a beat. Only in my wildest dreams could I have experienced this moment with Marcus. So many nights I have woken from a dream only to wish to be asleep. He had become just as much a part of my life as anyone else I knew. But now my dreams were real, standing here before me, and I was finally able to reach out and touch this mirage that was branded so deep within my soul. My attraction toward Marcus was multifaceted, for it wasn't only his flawless appearance that drew me in, but his noble character as well. He was the most caring, honorable person I had ever met. And unfortunately for Ryan's sake, the timing couldn't have been worse. Marcus's selfless example shed an even brighter light on Ryan's flawed integrity. He wasn't anywhere to be seen at my birthday or hospital bedside. And he certainly wasn't heroically jumping into treacherous waters or following me through dark cliffsides. No, Ryan paved the road that he had chosen for himself, and it cost him our relationship. My faithful eyes that once looked to him for comfort and strength began to look to someone else. He slowly disappeared from the plans of the future and was replaced by the man who visited me in my dreams.

I looked away from Marcus's inquisitive stare and slowly shook my head. His offer was enticing, and under different circumstances, I would've jumped at the chance to get to know him better. But I knew I couldn't. The fact remained that I was still engaged. And as far as Ryan knew, I was solely committed to him. It would only be fair to break things off with him first before pursuing a relationship with someone else. Not only for my sake but for Marcus's sake as well. He needed a clean slate just as much as I did. And Ryan needed a real taste of what it felt like to be honest in a difficult situation. He needed to see for himself that I remained faithful, despite the desire that lurked at my door. Our relationship was riddled with errors, but it was still together.

Oh, Ryan, what happened to you?

My heart unexpectedly ached at the thought of total severance. Perhaps the greater part of my being longed for our relationship to pull through our recent troubles.

Perhaps I still loved him . . .

A guttural noise sounded as Marcus cleared his throat to speak. "I don't know if you remember the first day we met, but I think about it all the time. I remember when I asked you what you were doing at that remote beach, and you said you were doing a little thinking. I asked you what you were thinking about, and you never got a chance to tell me. I can't tell you how many times I've wondered what you would've said if we had more time to talk. I figured I'd never see you again to ask. But now you're here, and well, as fate would have it, here's my chance. So, Gwendolyn, what were you thinking about?"

I looked at him dumbfounded as his question caught me off guard. I couldn't put into words what was going through my mind that day. I remembered being upset about Emma's disappearance. I was disturbed by her mother's hostility at the sheriff's meeting, and Ryan's indifference put a strain on our relationship. I needed a place to sort things out, and the beach just happened to be there. But what exactly I was thinking of as I walked the sands of the shore was for some reason lost. I was beginning to resent my memory that was showing to be so unreliable. And where was my rational judgment? Another absurd decision to take a walk under unfavorable circumstances. I never would've explored some unknown trail so late in the day. Come to think of it, I would've never decided to go swimming in my clothes either. No wonder

Marcus wondered what was going through my head when we met. He found me washed up on the shore! That's twice he's discovered I was either drowning or possibly washed up from drowning. He must think I'm crazy.

I think I'm crazy!

The split-second recollection of that moment brought a flood of embarrassment. If I was starting to care for this person in an intimate way, I certainly didn't want him digging around in uncharted territory I couldn't explain. He would consider me irrational and be scared off the trail for sure. I suddenly became uncomfortable as the hot poke of integrity prodded within my being. Even though I desperately wanted to make up a fictitious answer to appease his interest, I knew I couldn't. If there was to be any potential for a future with this man, I needed to start our relationship with a foundation of honesty. I took a deep breath and reluctantly decided to tell the truth.

"I'm really sorry to disappoint you, but I don't remember what I was thinking about. I needed a place to be by myself, and I happened to be in the area of that beach. I remember sitting in my car and feeling an overwhelming urge to take a walk. But after that, my memory fades. I know you're probably wondering why I was lying there wet in my clothes and covered in sand. But to be completely honest with you, I don't even know myself. I don't know if I decided to take a swim or if I just fell in. I don't even remember getting into the water. It's like that part of my memory is missing somewhere." I hung my head in discouragement and sputtered out my breath. His expression transitioned from amusement to concern.

"I don't know what's wrong with me, Marcus. Maybe I was so preoccupied with my troubles that I absentmindedly went through all the motions of walking and swimming? That would make sense in theory, right? But what about tonight? I was standing here before you joined me, speculating why I would wake up from a deep sleep and decide to take a random stroll at midnight. I've done some pretty sporadic things in my life, but never anything like this. And it's not like I came out here to do anything important. I came out here to think. And I don't even remember what about! I can't recollect waking up and making that decision. It was like someone made it for me." I covered my face with my hands and wished to disappear. At that moment, I hid behind the closed door of my heart and listened to the colliding waves that surrounded my dark world. I feared I shared too much. And I detested my resolve to be so honest. I wished I would have given him a quick made-up answer, and we would be talking about something else. I uncovered my face and was thankful he didn't run.

"I'm sorry," I said finally. "I'm sorry I shared so much. You wanted to know what I was thinking when we first met. Well, to answer your question, I don't know. I bet you think I'm crazy now." I wanted to break free from our conversation and cower under the nearest rock I could find. I looked to the ground and braced myself for an outpouring of laughter and questions.

But I received neither.

"No, Gwendolyn. I don't think you're crazy. I think you're very brave for admitting all of that to me. I feel honored you would trust me with such an intimate part of your life. I also think you need to cut yourself a break. I'm sure it is as you say, you were preoccupied with your troubles, and you absent-mindedly made decisions you usually wouldn't make. We've all done that before. There's nothing wrong with making a few sporadic decisions. And making a few mistakes. You're human. You should be allowed some room for error. And hey, if you didn't come to the beach, you wouldn't've met me. So for that, I'm grateful." His face suddenly became serious.

I quickly looked up as his unexpected comment awoke a network of emotions that slept within my breast. The air all at once became static. He took a small step forward and stopped within inches of my face. My skin bristled in expectancy. He slowly reached forward and caressed the side of one cheek. His reassuring eyes looked into mine and then down to my parted lips. I licked them several times and swallowed.

"I told you I came here after work to do a little thinking, too. But I never got a chance to tell you what I was thinking about. Would you like to know what it was?"

I wanted to open my mouth to answer, but nervous tension clamped it shut. My eyes broke from his stare to the side of his neck, where a throbbing vein pulsed in sync with my own. My head slowly bobbed up and down.

"I was thinking about you, Gwendolyn. I can't get you out of my head. Ever since we first met, I knew there was something special about you. It's like I found the missing piece to my soul, and I can't bear the thought of letting you go. I almost lost you once. I can't let that happen again." His hand reached forward to cup my other cheek. He gently pulled my face into his. I drank in the heady smell of cologne and sweat that intoxicated my soul like wine.

"I've waited for you all my life," he breathed, barely audible above the pounding in my ears. His black eyes lifted to study mine.

He suddenly leaned forward and pressed his lips hard to mine in a kiss. All the world around me faded as his eager mouth covered every inch of mine. His hands were gentle yet powerful, kneading deep into my hair and pulling me in close. For a few precious minutes, our souls intertwined as the building desires we both shared were finally fulfilled. He pulled his head back from his drunken state and uttered something inaudible.

"Don't make me do this," he mouthed, brushing his lips against the surface of my own. "Don't make me do this."

"Don't make you do what?" I murmured, opening my eyes briefly. I hooked my hands around the back of his neck and tugged him in for another kiss. He gave in to the draw of my mouth and struggled to break free.

"Don't make me . . . don't make me fall in love with you."

The magic roller-coaster of sheer euphoria came to a screeching halt. I quickly broke from our embrace and looked at him square in the face. His eyes were wide and darting. His face was pale and haunted with fear. The kiss that led to insurmountable elation now had me utterly confused.

"What's so wrong with loving me?" I asked, suddenly hurt.

He took a few steps back and nervously ran his fingers through his sweaty hair. He opened his mouth as if he wanted to say something, but then shut it. I studied his eyes and waited for him to answer the question that visibly plagued his contentment. It was his turn now to be uncomfortable.

"I know what you're thinking, but you're wrong," he said finally. "It's not you. Well, yes, it's you. But it's not anything you've done wrong. It's what you're doing right. You make me feel something I can't control." His eyes squinted at his spoken words and then closed. A series of muscles pulled within his chest as he tilted his head toward the sky. "I can't help the way I feel when I'm around you, and that scares me. I don't know how to give myself to someone wholeheartedly. And I don't want to get hurt. I told you not to make me fall in love with you because I've never loved anyone before. You would be my first." His eyes clouded, and a look of puzzlement took over. He turned his face away.

I stepped in closer and studied the magnificent creature that awkwardly paced in my presence. This couldn't be true! This man, who happened to be the most beautiful person I've ever met in my whole life, has never loved? False! There was no flaw to be found in his person. None in his face. None in his physique. None in his personality. None! And judging from his appearance, I would guess he was in his mid-twenties. To say a man of that age and such caliber has never loved? That was really hard to believe. Women would jump at the chance to get him to even look in their direction.

"But you're wrong," he blurted out, interrupting my train of thought as if I spoke it out loud. "You think because you find me attractive that others have claimed my heart. But I haven't given it away. To me, a pretty girl is just that. A pretty girl. A body or a face. An empty shell. It's all superficial. I want what's inside the package, not just the wrapping paper around the box. I see something in you that I've never seen before . . . and I'm attracted to what I see." His eyes became ignited, and he stepped in closer to grasp my hand. He pressed his hot cheek against the surface of my skin before kissing it lightly. "It's you, Gwendolyn. It's all about you."

I averted my eyes from his bowed head as a wash of embarrassment flooded my face. I fumbled to find my voice and thanked him for the compliment that ravished my heart.

"I want to get to know this missing puzzle piece of mine," he whispered, talking into my hand. He turned it over and began tracing the outline of my palm with his finger. "Do you think I can get your number before the night is over?"

I drew back my hand in sudden alarm. The mention of time cut through the moment like a knife. I looked to the sky and was thankful for the moon that was still just as bright. The conversation with Marcus caused me to completely forget the urgency to return home.

"Yes. Of course, you can have my number. Only, I have to get home. I'm very sorry to leave so soon. If my parents wake up and find me missing, I will worry them for sure. Do you have a cell phone to take my number?"

"No. But I have a pen and paper. You can never be too prepared for work." He reached into his back pocket and pulled out a small pad of paper.

I quickly scribbled my number and smiled. "I hope to hear from you soon."

He looked down at the number and pressed the notepad to his chest. "You will."

Chapter Eight

She had no idea what kind of hold she had over me.

I stood there and watched as her tiny form disappeared over the tall, grassy hill. I would've never expected for things to turn out this way. What an unforeseen event to happen. Me? Fall in love? The balance of power had suddenly shifted. The impossible has proven itself to be wrong. And yet, I was thankful that it did, for I was deeply honored to receive such a gift. A beautiful spirit has unexpectedly graced my presence. She was so innocent—so pure. I could sit with her all night and watch as her thoughts entered her lovely head. Her mind was filled with such complexity. It was like a dripping honeycomb—so sweet to my taste. I couldn't get enough! The captivating thought of her soul sent a shiver down my spine. I buttoned my shirt with quivering fingers and stood at the water's edge.

She had me trembling in her presence.

Me! This valiant man of power. How could these strong arms go so limp at the slightest touch of her finger? I was either weaker than I thought, or I didn't have a clear understanding of what love's true power could do. I looked down at my feet and took a few steps back. A wave extended far enough to cover the tops of my shoes. I steadied my stance on drier sand and drew in the salty air.

She's worth it, though.

And I don't care if I get hurt. I'm willing to take the risk. I've always longed to experience the emotion of love. To be able to hold someone in my arms and know they love me in return. This girl is the one I chose!

If she would only give me a chance.

I closed my eyes and attempted to conjure an image of her presence. I could still see her face as if it were etched in my mind.

(The sea pulled back and pushed forward, revealing a mysterious shadow that bobbed in the distance.)

Milky white skin that would flush pink when she saw me. Thick blonde hair that cascaded to the small of her back. Full, glossy lips that tasted so sweet. And her eyes . . . her emerald green eyes that were as innocent as they were unnerving.

(A large foaming wave crashed onto the shore, spilling a dark silhouette that coiled in the sand.)

I put my hand to my pocket and checked to see if my notepad was still there. I had to see her again. Just one more chance to kiss her delicate mouth. Only this time, I won't cut our kiss so short.

(The shadowy form that twisted on the shore slowly mounted to a cobra-like stance.)

I smiled at the thought of her velvety soft skin and opened my eyes.

Avangeline was lifted in all of her glory and was eagerly waiting for my acknowledgment. Her lacy fins fanned wide as they greedily clenched for the driest patches of sand to give her more stability. A long muscle pulled in her belly as she leaned back on her massive tail and smiled.

"So, what did I miss?" she asked nonchalantly. She grasped a handful of auburn curls and swept them across one shoulder, revealing two perfectly rounded breasts that shimmered in the moonlight. Her spreading fins suddenly erected her body high. A tumbling wave washed in, plastering sand across her scaled underside. Her face looked down at the water in annoyance and then back up at me.

"You didn't miss anything. Put your worries at ease. Everything is going exactly to plan."

"What do you mean everything is going exactly to plan?" she hissed. "Were you able to distract her from him?"

I didn't have to see her face to know her eyes burned with expectancy. I looked down at my shoes as another wave rolled in and soaked them. "Yes. I believe I did. But what about you? How far do you think he is from being . . . enraptured?" I knew the question was a perfect diversion as it would certainly spark the streak of pride that ran deep within her veins.

Her ruby lips curved to a cynical sneer. "How far do you think I've come? Marcus, I was able to show myself completely to him without any water to hide my form, and he was still interested! Can you believe that? You should've seen his eyes looking me over like I was some treasure he unearthed. He even asked to touch my tail!" She spread the delicate folds of her pearly fins and fanned them in sarcasm. She gave a confident laugh and declared, "He's enraptured with me all right. I just need one more meeting to . . . shall we say, finalize things. Well, you know what I'm talking about."

I looked down at the sand and shook my head. Her flippant comment struck an unforeseen chord. She looked at her own squirming body and began picking off the rocks that were glued to her silvery scales. She turned her tail to one side and grunted in frustration when a new area of pebbles was revealed.

"It's just so hard because I have no way of getting a hold of him." She picked off a stubborn stone and threw it. "I come out here every day, but he hasn't visited for a while. I guess that's where you come in, right?" She paused from her grooming and looked up at me with wide, foreboding eyes. I had complete control in this situation, and she knew it.

"Right. That's where I come in. But listen, I want to make sure she doesn't love him first before you take over. I mean, they are still engaged. They loved each other enough to pledge their lives together forever. I know this form of bonding doesn't make any sense to you, but it can be pretty powerful." I thought of my own vulnerability for a second. "I can influence her to invite him to come out here. That part is easy. But I don't want her to blindly make a decision she will regret for the rest of her life. I'm finding she's a really special person, and I don't want her to suffer at my expense."

Her composed face suddenly contorted with anger. She towered high above the shoreline and slapped her tail hard against the sand. The loud smack sounded throughout the beach.

"Marcus! What happened to you? Are you joking?"

"No. I'm not."

"Do you mean to tell me that you care for this . . . this . . . this thing?" she sputtered. She spat on the ground and turned her face from mine.

I suppressed the anger that her comment released and pushed my hands deeper into my pockets. I knew what it felt like to be on the other side of the water. I understood the assumptions that were made for a lack of facts. I also understood the animalistic hostility that a living environment could create. Avangeline knew no other way because it was simply a part of her nature. She was, after all, part animal.

"She's not a thing, Avangeline. She's a person. And, yes, I care for her."

"So, what does that mean for me? Should I just abandon all hope because you don't want her to get hurt? What about hurting me? Have you thought about how selfish it would be to take our plan to the very end and not let me finish it? You said we were going to do this together. Or have you changed your mind? I guess time and land have caused you to forget your best friend who still lives in the water."

"I said I would help you, and I stand by my word. I just want to go about things in a different way, that's all."

"I'm listening." Her eyes gravitated to a piece of seaweed that was woven in her hair, and she yanked it out.

"Instead of me influencing her to bring him to you, why don't I just tell her to do so?"

Her jaw dropped while her fierce eyes scanned mine for humor. Astonishment took over as my serious expression proved I wasn't joking. I lifted my hand to stop any future outbursts from being hurled.

"Just listen to me. There's something different about her. She's not like anyone I've ever met. She's not only given me a new outlook on humanity, but a new outlook on myself. I want to be honest with her and tell her everything. If I put the decision in her hands, she will more than likely see things our way. And I think she will appreciate the choice to do so. I can easily influence her to bring him out to you. Heck, if you think he's ready, I can easily influence him to come out to you."

"Then why don't you?!" she shrieked.

"Because I don't want to hurt her. If she still loves him, I will always know I played a part in her pain. And I would like to someday think we could have a future together. A future with no deceptions or influences. Just her accepting me for what I—" I couldn't finish my sentence because a low chuckle cut me short.

"I can't believe what I'm hearing right now. I can't believe it! Just to make sure this isn't all some nightmare, I think I need to ask the obvious. Marcus, are you telling me you love her?"

I remained silent.

"I can't believe this! You love her? That's the most absurd thing I've ever heard. Do you really think she will love you back? After the mirage has faded and she is left with your real self, do you really think she will stand by your side? Do you think she will hear the truth about who you are and not hate you for it? Marcus, those . . . those beasts cannot be trusted. You've seen their hypocrisy. They're selfish and insensitive. They care for no one else but themselves."

"Yes, I understand all that. But as I said before, she's different from all the others." The patience I once had for her insensitivity was beginning to wear thin.

"Do you think because you stand on two legs that you are now one of them? You will always be what you are, no matter what changes have taken place. Don't you forget that!" Her tail pushed hard against the sand as she snaked herself to where I stood. Her hand reached for mine and then lowered. "Marcus, I say these things because I care for you. I've always seen our relationship as the foundation of my life. I don't want to see you get hurt over some rash decision to be honest. If you give your heart away, she will crush you. Mark my words, she will not understand who you are. I guarantee it. You will meet me here on this very shore and tell me I was right." Her empty eyes longed for mine to agree.

"Then that's just the risk I'm willing to take," I said firmly. I turned to give her my back and looked at the sky that was beginning to brighten.

I could easily bring Ryan out to Avangeline and pretend as if I knew nothing. I would appease Avangeline in doing so, and I would appease myself. The girl of my dreams would have no strings attached. We would live our lives happily together in love. After all, I was the better choice for her than that filthy wretch who called himself a man. But in the end, what would that make me? A liar. I could never kiss her lips again knowing that mine were covered with deceit. No, I would always know the truth behind our relationship, and it would eat me alive. This choice was one she would have to make for herself.

Him or me.

My decision to tell her could be no clearer.

"So, what if she still loves him? Huh? What if she won't invite him out here because she's still attached? Is that it then? Should I just assume our plan is finished, and my future now hangs in the balance of chance? Do you know how hard it's been for me to build a relationship with this man? You got lucky, Marcus. You got out quick because your victim was weak. But my situation hasn't been that easy. It's taken me time. It's taken well-spoken words. It's taken the right body movements. It's taken countless dreams of becoming freed. And now it's possible that all my hard work has been in vain?"

"No. Don't think like that. I highly doubt she will still love him after she hears the truth about her relationship."

"And what if her heart deceives her? What if she thinks she feels nothing for him, but deep down she's still subconsciously in love? Have you ever considered that? What if she commits the ultimate trespass of giving a loved one over to me by choice? Are you prepared to watch her suffer the consequences of that decision? Or, better put, are you prepared to suffer the regret of knowing you inflicted those consequences?"

Her question flung through the air and pierced me between heart and spirit. I spun around and scanned the heartless face that waited for my response.

"That . . . that won't happen."

"Oh really? Well, don't deceive yourself. You know as well as I do that anything can happen within a human. Their hearts are deep and unsearchable. Who can know its depths? If they can't understand their own ways, and it comes from within their being, how can we? Do you really think you know all there is to know about love? Have you ever considered why a woman's heart beats within her breast for a man she desires? Or why a man holds a woman close and pledges his life for hers? Can you understand why they suddenly change their minds as if nothing was shared between them? What happens to that bond you tell me I don't understand? I've surveyed above this ocean for all my life. I've seen more than you give me credit for. I've watched the proposals and the marriages. I've witnessed the joyous celebrations of the happy couples that are united as one flesh. But I've also seen the other side of it all. I've listened as they bitterly separate. I've experienced what it feels like, first-hand, to have someone break the trust that was built within a relationship and discard it away as if it were a worthless piece of trash. And let me tell you, it isn't to be desired. You are giving it all to her. You are putting all of your faith into one frail person . . ." She straightened her shoulders with an icy stare. "And you will regret it."

Her tail spun in a wide semicircle as she whipped her body around toward the ocean. She shook her head and cursed while she slowly slithered back to sea.

"For your sake, I hope she doesn't let you down," she called over her shoulder. She approached the water's edge and turned around. "Look, I don't care what you do or how you do it! All I want is to stand on this shore with my own two feet. I grow weary of this watery prison I'm forced to call home." She gave me one last frown before propelling through the sand and diving into the water.

Chapter Nine

"Just call me when you get this message. I have something really important to talk to you about. Okay, well . . . that's it. I hope to hear from you soon."

I muttered a string of obscenities and paced at my bedroom window. Marcus would be arriving any minute, and my time to talk to Ryan was running out. Like always, I was unable to reach him. A typical occurrence that hardly fazed me these days. Only this time it was crucial for me to get a hold of him as soon as possible. My instantaneous date with Marcus had taken me by surprise. I was expecting to hear from him in a few days, three at least. He didn't even wait twenty-four hours before he called to meet again. I was so excited to hear his voice that I completely forgot about my pending commitment to Ryan. By the time I realized I had neglected its severance, it was too late to call and postpone. Marcus never left a phone number in case I needed to reach him. So, the window of time to break things off had suddenly closed, and I was left scrambling, hoping to contact somebody I knew was as elusive as he was inconsiderate. In the worst-case scenario, I could tell Marcus our relationship was nearly over. But that wasn't how I wanted to start things off.

I looked out my window one last time and walked to my full-length mirror. I smoothed back my hair that fell to my waist and dabbed on a bit more lip gloss. My eyes wandered to my metallic flats, and I quickly ripped them off my feet. A brown-heeled boot would pair better with jeans and would give an extra inch in height. But if I decided to change my shoes, I needed to change my blouse as well. I grunted in frustration as the inspection of my outfit made its third round, and I stripped my top to the ground. After stepping over the growing pile of clothes on the floor, I scrambled to find its replacement. My eyes searched while I combed through the tangled mess of hangers before reluctantly settling on a pale pink sweater. I approached the full-length mirror again and turned in a small circle. I wasn't completely confident in my appearance, but my outfit would have to do.

I didn't know why I felt so insecure when I was around Marcus. I wasn't a prideful person when it came to my looks, but I wasn't self-conscious about them either. Perhaps I was intimidated because he was simply better-looking than I was. Just a glance at his physique sent color to my cheeks. But a part of me felt very exposed when his eyes held mine. There were moments within our conversation when I could feel him watching me in fascination. It was like I was some new breed of animal he had never seen before. Every word I spoke, he hung on. Every movement I made, he scrutinized.

Every emotion I felt, he sympathized with. His interest in me was very evident. Unlike Ryan, who wouldn't even give me eye contact half the time, Marcus's eyes were deep and penetrating, and when they searched my face, it was like he was looking into my soul. I just hoped he wouldn't be disappointed if he looked too closely.

I jumped from my pose in the mirror when a deep hum of a black sports car sounded from our driveway. I grabbed my cell phone from my dresser and switched the setting to vibrate. The last thing I needed was a phone call from Ryan to spoil our first date. I gave my reflection a final glance and slipped outside my door.

As I approached the bottom of the staircase, I could hear the worried voice of my father rise above the hushed of my mother's.

"But who is he, Carol?" he pressed.

"He's the young man who saved her life on her birthday."

"Yes, but what about Ryan?"

My mother didn't have a chance to respond as my entrance to the living room broke the anxious murmuring. Both sets of eyes watched in concern while I drew close to their quiet huddle.

"Honey, who is this Marcus? And what about Ryan? Aren't you two still engaged?"

"Yes, Dad. We are. But we're not doing very well. I'm sorry I can't explain the details right now, but I will tonight."

"Well, how long have you known him? And what does he think about God?"

"I don't know what he thinks about God. We haven't talked about life like that yet."

A sharp knock at the door sounded down the hall.

"Daddy, please," I whispered. "Please trust me on this. You know I wouldn't go out with just anyone. Marcus is a really nice person. He hasn't given me any reason to question his character otherwise. We're just going out to get a quick bite to eat, that's all. It's really no big deal."

The etched lines in his forehead deepened as he listened to my rationalizing.

"And please don't say anything about Ryan. It's not like I'm trying to hide our relationship or anything. I was planning to tell Marcus about him tonight. I would've preferred to tell him sooner. I just haven't had enough time."

Another knock at the door sent my eyes pleading.

"I just want to make sure you're making the right decisions, honey. What does he do for a living to drive a sports car?" He shook his head. "Never mind. That doesn't matter now. I won't say anything about Ryan if you don't want me to." He gave my head a parting kiss and walked down the hall.

I smiled at my mother, who shifted uncomfortably in her stance. She looked just as nervous as I was.

"Hello, Marcus. Please come in."

A tall figure stepped through the doorway, and my dad slowly closed the door behind him.

Oh! Please don't grill him with questions!

"Hello, sir. It's a privilege to finally meet you," Marcus's controlled voice greeted. My father shook his hand in formality and led him down the hall. He stepped into the living room, and my mother softly gasped. She recognized the same thing I did when I first saw him—beauty.

"Hello, ma'am. Nice to meet you. Hello, Gwendolyn."

"Hey," I managed to say. I glanced at his face, half-way expecting to see the panicked look of a trapped rabbit. Interrogations from protective fathers would make any man's palms sweat. He didn't even know my last name to address my parents properly. But his commanding appearance seemed unshaken.

"Marcus, you can call me Mr. Hart. And let me start off by thanking you for saving our daughter's life. Your compassionate act of heroism has given us an extra reason to count our blessings."

"The decision to save her life could've been no clearer," he said, taking a slight bow. "And I would do it again if I needed to."

"What an impressive thing to say, given you could've lost your life. I hope you didn't suffer any injury."

"Yes, I've worried for you myself," my mother voiced softly. "Every night, I've said a prayer for the kind gentleman who risked his life for my baby girl. When I saw the extent of Gwendolyn's injuries, I could only imagine what discomfort you were experiencing. The doctor who helped us at the hospital said you needed to be seen. He also mentioned a guardian angel must have been watching over her because you saved her just in—" Her voice broke, and her face reddened in grief. The incident was too fresh to be completely healed with time. She turned her head toward the kitchen to conceal her weakened emotions. My father smoothed her hand to help her finish. "I'm sorry for getting choked up. I'm just so grateful you were there to help."

"Don't be sorry for crying, Mrs. Hart. I'm grateful I was there to help, too. I knew something was wrong when I saw her stranded on the rocks. I debated to rush over while I waited for her to make it down to safety. By the time I realized she needed my assistance, she had already fallen into the water." He looked down at me and smiled. "She's a pretty special treasure to lose. I understand your anguish completely. And, to answer your question, Mr. Hart, no. I didn't get hurt too badly. Maybe a few scratches here and there. But nothing to see a doctor for."

I looked at my father, who slowly unfolded his arms from his chest. The pressure in the room was beginning to lessen.

"Well, I'm glad to hear that!" my father declared. "How fortunate you are that you didn't get hurt. And what a blessing it is to finally meet you so we can show our gratitude. Thank you, Marcus."

"It's an honor, sir."

"So, getting back to tonight. What time were you planning to bring Gwen home?"

"I'll answer your question if you'll answer mine. What time do you want her home?"

"Good response! Eleven o'clock will be just fine. And if the night runs any later, all I ask is that you call. We've had some trouble in our neighborhood a few months back that has caused us all to be a little wary. Gwendolyn's good friend has been missing, and the police are presuming she's dead. She went out one night and just vanished. So, a simple phone call to let us know where you are will put our minds at ease."

"Oh, how awful. I'm so sorry to hear about your loss," Marcus said, frowning in my direction. "The last thing I want is to worry you unnecessarily, Mr. Hart. I'll make sure to bring her home on time. And if the night runs late, even a minute past eleven, I give you my word that we'll call you immediately."

My parents made eye contact with each other and nodded, seeming pleased. Their form of silent communication revealed a steady evolvement of mutual approval.

"Well, you guys better go and enjoy your date," my father announced, ushering us to the door. "It was nice meeting you, Marcus."

"Yes, I'm glad I can put a face to a name now. Such a pleasure to finally meet you," my mother called.

I held my creeping smile as I silently followed my parents through the living room and down the hall. The cloud of trepidation that encompassed the room only minutes ago had lifted. With a few well-spoken words, my father confidently released me into Marcus's care. No further questions asked. It was nothing short of a miracle.

***

For the majority of the ride into town, we sat in silence as we wove our way through the busy streets of GlenPoint. It was early for a Friday evening, and the streets were already packed with cars. I surveyed the sights as the restaurants, shops, and droves of people standing at street corners passed by my window. We merged into a congested lane that stretched for several blocks and headed for the heart of the city. The destination of where we were going was uncertain, but one thing I knew for sure—I wanted nothing more than to be with Marcus. I took in a deep breath that smelled of leather and musk and turned to the man who powered the muscle. My eyes scanned timidly as they took in his every detail.

He was so perfect.

For the first time since meeting him, I was able to stare without any reservation. And I couldn't get my fill. The muscles in his arms flexed tight as he slowed his car to a stop. Several people waiting at an intersection stepped out into the street and crossed. He ran his fingers through his slicked-back hair and smiled. He knew I was staring.

"You look beautiful tonight," he said, breaking the silence.

We made eye contact for a nervous second before he focused back on the street.

"Thank you. You look beautiful . . . I mean handsome, too."

He glanced in my direction and started to chuckle. "Are you okay?"

"Trust me, I'm great. I'm just really nervous right now. But at least I'm sitting in an upright position this time. I have to say, your car looks totally different from the front seat."

His broad chest filled deeply with air, and he gave a hearty laugh. "Wow! That makes me feel a whole lot better. I've been struggling here for the past eight minutes trying to figure out how to start a conversation. I finally have my chance to get to know you better, and I can't even string a few words together to make a sentence. It's so easy to talk when we're in passing. But to actually be on a date with you . . . well, that's a different story. I guess I have to take this one step at a time."

"Yes, I'm afraid you're right," I agreed. "I've been anxious about our date ever since we hung up the phone."

"That makes two of us." He sighed, seeming more relaxed. "Okay. So, we're both a little nervous. At least we're in the same boat. Let's start off by figuring out where we want to go for dinner. What kind of food are you in the mood for? Take your pick of any restaurant here on the strip, and I'll take you to it. Or we can venture somewhere out of Glen Point. It's totally up to you."

"You know, now that we're being honest with each other, I have to admit I'm not very hungry. My nerves and my appetite pretty much go hand in hand. But I can nibble on something small while you eat. What are you in the mood for?"

"Nothing either. Can you believe that? It's too bad we can't find a place to just sit and talk. We can always order food if we get hungry." He stopped at a red light.

The car became quiet again as the unforeseen predicament posed an awkward dilemma. His blinker light clicked softly while he waited for the light to change.

"Hey, I have an idea. Why don't I take you to my work? It doesn't open until seven, so we'll beat all the crowds. It's the perfect place to sit and get to know one another. And it's close to your house, so we won't have to travel. The best part is there's no pressure to order any food. If we get hungry, I can simply have the chef prepare us something. He should be there by now doing his prep work . . ." He checked the time on his watch and nodded. "Yeah, he's there."

"But can we do that? I mean, can we just drop in and hang out if it's not open?"

"Sure. Why not? If I'm not mistaken, he's preparing duck, lamb, and Chilean sea bass tonight. There's also appetizers and things we can munch on if you're not too fond of those choices."

"No, that sounds great. I would love to visit La Mer. That's its name, right?"

"Right. It means 'the sea'. Fittingly put for where it's located."

He made a quick U-turn at the finalization of our decision and followed the road back to GlenPoint Strip. The start-and-stop lane of traffic had us stranded behind a slow-moving camper. His jaw slowly clenched as he waited for the vacationer to move forward. "You know, I was really disturbed when your father told me about your friend who's been missing. I can't imagine what it must feel like to lose someone so unexpectedly. Were you close to her?"

My face flinched in response to his dreaded question. "Yes. I was. She was my best friend for seven years. But she was lost before she went missing. I mean, she was lost in her spirit before she was reported missing physically. We weren't getting along very well toward the end of our relationship. It made the whole situation a lot easier to cope with." I chewed on my bottom lip and looked outside my window. I didn't want Emma to have any part in this moment. Perhaps I felt the need to guard Marcus because her complications angered my former fiancé. I quickly sought for a way to redirect our conversation.

"I didn't mean to bring up something so painful." He paused at a stop sign. "We don't have to talk about her if you don't want to. I just wanted to let you know I'm here for you if you ever need to talk." He turned from the road and looked at me sympathetically.

I made eye contact with him and smiled. "Thank you for saying that. You have no idea how much it means to me that you're so considerate of my problems."

"It will always be my pleasure."

I fidgeted with the hem of my sweater, and he looked back to the road.

"So, do you live here in GlenPoint?" I asked, trying to change the subject.

He shifted in his seat and drove a little faster. "Yes, I do. I just moved here a few months ago."

"Oh, really? Where did you move from?"

His eyes quickly darted as La Mer's dimly lit parking lot suddenly came into view. He pulled the car into the first available parking space and shut the engine off.

"Well, we're here," he announced.

I never ate at The Silver Fox Steak House. The lack of curb appeal and subpar food ratings kept me from its doors. And the consistent empty parking lot proved I wasn't alone in my opinion. Even the local newspaper reviewed the restaurant as needing a bit of refinement. Our town became excited when it finally went out of business. Rumors promised a small shopping center would eventually replace the gigantic eyesore. To everyone's surprise, a mysterious sign announcing La Mer's grand opening was posted shortly after its closing. The unknown establishment had quite an undertaking, as the building needed more than a resurrection of a reputation. And I wasn't sure if it was headed in the right direction. Judging from the outside, the large brick building appeared to be nothing more than an average hangout. But when the double doors opened wide, I quickly reconsidered my opinion.

La Mer was breathtaking.

Lavish tapestries of crimson and plum covered each wall, giving it an immediate feeling of luxury and warmth. A large crystal chandelier hung high above a wooden dance floor, with several tables surrounding it throughout. There was a bar romantically arrayed with candles and fresh flowers, and gold velvet chairs stretched far into the recesses. The air was perfumed with exotic smells of incense and prepared meats and was strangely awakening my slumbering appetite. The servers of the club moved to the steady bass of music while they quickly arranged the tables for seating. Some were folding linen napkins neatly into triangles while others were setting silverware and plates. One of them stopped in his folding and watched as we walked into the room. Marcus turned to me and extended his hand with a smile. A feeling of warmth spread up my arm when his fingers slowly closed around mine.

"So, what do you think?"

"What do I think? Marcus, I think it's beautiful!" My eyes widened, taking it all in.

"Do you really? That means a lot to hear you say that. I'm pretty proud of it myself. And it didn't always look like this, you know. It took a lot of work to get it where it is today. I think it turned out okay."

"Turned out okay? The Silver Fox Steak House was rumored to be one of the worst restaurants in the city. I'm surprised they didn't tear the building down after it went out of business. I could've never imagined something so attractive was hidden beneath such a plain exterior."

"But that's what makes it so unique, don't you think? I'm sure most people drive past it, assuming it's rundown because of its previous owner. And that's such a shame because everything deserves a second chance. Beauty can come from the ugliest places sometimes."

He spun around as a tall, ruddy server tapped him on the shoulder. The timid man quietly excused himself for interrupting our conversation and asked how to arrange a bouquet of orchids that were displayed at the front desk. Marcus motioned with his hands how large he envisioned the arrangement, noting that he wanted several other flowers to be added to the vase. The server bowed with an apology and quickly disappeared from sight. Marcus frowned as he watched the waiter leave.

"I'm sorry for that. Let's go find a table so we can get our night started. How about one in the back of the room? It offers more privacy."

"Sure. That sounds great."

"Good."

We wove our way through the shadowed dining area, where he selected a small table hidden in the corner. I thanked him for his courtesy as he pulled out my chair and guided me to the golden pillow. He reached for a lighter from his back pocket and quickly lit the tea light that was centered on the table. He then took his seat across from mine and breathed a sigh of satisfaction.

"So, here we are," he uttered, looking into my face.

"Yes, here we are."

Light from the candle flickered across his face, making his eyes appear as black as night. They took in my every detail while they darted from my eyes, to my hair, to my cheeks, to my lips. He leaned back in his chair and crossed his legs under the table.

"Please tell me about yourself, Gwendolyn. Start at the beginning. I want to know everything. Your likes. Your dislikes. Your triumphs. And your fears. Who is this person that I think of day and night?"

I swept away my hair that fell in my face and shifted nervously in my chair. I didn't know what to say. I wasn't comfortable to speak freely and welcome lengthy silences when they came. How was I going to have a relationship with this man if I couldn't carry a conversation with him? I hated this crippling insecurity!

"No pressure, by the way," he added with a smile.

"Well . . . I just graduated from GlenPoint High School. My family and I moved about—"

My sentence was suddenly interrupted as a heavyset man dressed in a white chef's coat quickly approached our table. His wide eyes met Marcus's as he took a deep bow.

"Please excuse me, sir. I'm very sorry for interrupting your evening, but I wanted to—"

"Just a minute, Mike," Marcus said, not looking up. "Gwendolyn, will you excuse us for a minute, please?"

"Sure, no problem." I nodded and smiled at the sweaty-faced cook who looked like he wanted to run.

"What is it?" Marcus asked.

"I'm very sorry for interrupting you, sir. I just wanted to ask how many cases of champagne you would like me to order for next week's party. The reservation just changed to a head count of ninety-two."

Marcus grunted and quickly stood to his feet. The pair walked a few paces from our table and discussed competitive prices for the order.

I was thankful for the unexpected interruption as it gave me ample time to prepare my answer. I made a mental list of all the hobbies I enjoyed when a loud vibration sounded from my purse. I unhooked its strap from the back of my chair and hesitantly pulled out my cell phone. Ryan's phone number was displayed on the caller's identification. I quickly shut it off and stuffed it back in my bag. At that moment, I knew what I needed to share first.

"I'm so sorry about these interruptions," Marcus stated, taking his seat. "Maybe coming to work wasn't such a hot idea after all. Let's just hope it doesn't happen again."

"No problem. I understand completely." I smiled weakly and swallowed, feeling as though I needed to throw up.

"Okay, so where did we leave off? Ah, yes. You were saying you just graduated from GlenPoint High School, and that your family moved to . . . What's the matter?"

"Oh, it's nothing," I answered softly. "I just remembered I have something really important to talk to you about."

"But are you okay? You look a little pale."

"That's because I've been dreading this moment ever since we hung up the phone. I have something really important to tell you, and I'm afraid it will either offend you or turn you off completely. I wish I didn't have to mention anything at all, but I want our relationship to start on the right note."

He reached across the table and covered my hand with his. "Hey, it's okay. Whatever it is you have to tell me, I won't be offended. I'm very grateful I've met such an honest person. You're thinking about our future. How can that be a bad thing? Besides, there isn't a single thing you can say that will turn me off." The grip of his hand gently tightened as he wove his fingers between mine.

I avoided his stare and looked at the wall behind him. An unexpected arrow of disgrace struck me right between the eyes.

I didn't deserve him.

I came to the table with too much baggage. This man had never been in a relationship before, and I haven't even ended mine.

"I promise you, I won't get angry. And I won't judge. Please don't fear me."

"You don't even know what I'm going to say, and you're already okay with it? Who does that?"

"Your future."

My future?

His eyes slowly fell from mine, and he respectfully gave me my space. My integrity was tarnished as far as he was concerned, and he still accepted me for who I was.

"I'm so glad I've met you, Marcus. Thank you for giving me such grace. And let me start off by saying that it was never my intention to be involved in this situation in the first place. I was hoping to resolve this issue before we had our date. But everything happened so suddenly that it left me no time." I took in a deep breath and held it until it burned. "Well, I guess I better tell you. Before you and I met, I—"

I was interrupted again as the twice-offending chef suddenly approached our table. His shaky hand held the front of his coat while he bowed at the waist in reverence.

"I'm . . . I'm v-v-v-very sorry, sir. But the order . . . f-f-f-for the party has just—"

The blubbering worker couldn't finish his sentence before Marcus raised his hand to stop him.

"Not now, Mike. I don't care what it is you have to say. Not now."

The chef's square jaw opened to speak, but suddenly clamped shut. And then, as if some invisible hand moved him against his will, he abruptly straightened in his posture and spun on his heel to leave. A subtle look of anger played across Marcus's face as he watched the dark figure robotically walk across the dance floor and disappear beyond view.

"Well, I guess there's no leaving work, is there?" He folded his hands across the table. His narrowed eyes softened, and he started to laugh. "I can't walk through that front door without getting attacked by a swarm of bees. You would think they would see me on a date with a beautiful girl and leave me alone for one minute. Then again, I've never been on a date with a beautiful girl before, so what do I know?"

"Can't somebody answer their questions for them? I mean, what's your job description here? Are you the head manager or something?"

"The head manager? No. I'm not the manager." He chuckled and became serious. "I own La Mer."

"You own it?"

I arched my eyebrow and shook my head in dismay. Surely he was joking. Judging from his appearance, he was no older than twenty. How could someone so young be so successful?

"Yes, I own it. But there are times, like tonight for example, that I wish I didn't."

"You own it? Are you serious? Wow! I guess that explains all the questions from staff members. I didn't put two and two together because you look so young. I don't know why I haven't asked this before, but how old are you?"

"I'm twenty-three. And I'm sure you're wondering how I wound up with all of . . . well this," he said, spreading his hands. "But I'm afraid I won't get very far in my explanation if we stay here much longer. Would it be okay with you if I took you to my apartment? It's located on the top floor of this building. We don't have to drive. And I can guarantee you, Mike won't interrupt us again."

I looked at him in shock as I couldn't get past the wealth of his possessions. All I could do was nod.

"Great. The staircase to my apartment is located at the back of the building. Let me take you to it."

He led me by the hand, and we made our way to the back of the club.

Chapter Ten

His apartment was small. Hardly an apartment for someone who had money. It was furnished with things necessary for living. A wooden table and chair in the kitchen. A lamp on a stand in the corner of the living room. A loveseat by the window. For the exception of a small cross hanging on the wall, the room was completely void of all personal expression. There were no pictures of family or friends. There were no colorful curtains or rugs. There wasn't even a television for entertainment. It was such a grand departure from the showy nightclub that paraded itself downstairs. La Mer was filled with life and indulgence. His living quarters were sterile and indifferent. It was baffling to me to see a man own so much and show so little. And yet, I was pleased to discover this humble side of Marcus. Until now, his mirror reflected impossible perfection. It put things back into proper perspective.

He was only human, like myself.

The wooden floor creaked loudly as he crossed to the back of the room to turn on a lamp. The dim light illuminated only a small crescent of space, leaving the rest of his apartment in shadows. He set his keys on the windowsill and called for me to enter.

"Come on in. Please make yourself at home. Can I offer you something to drink? Water, tea?"

"Oh, no thank you. I think I'm okay for now." I stepped in behind him and looked around for a place to sit. After considering his sparsely equipped room, I decided to remain standing. I didn't want to take the only chair available.

"Are you sure? I might have a can of soda somewhere in the back of the refrigerator."

"No, thank you. Really, I'm great."

"Well, okay. Let me know if you change your mind. I'll go grab my chair from the kitchen. Why don't you take the loveseat and get comfortable?" He disappeared behind the breakfast bar and reappeared with an old, straight-backed chair. I sat on the lumpy beige cushion and wiped my sweaty palms down the front of my lap. I was beginning to feel nervous again.

"Well, what a strange turn our date has taken. I pictured taking you to an elegant restaurant where we would dine on fine lobster and stare into each other's eyes by candlelight." He spread his hands in my direction. "I didn't think we would sit in my apartment with the hum of my refrigerator for our ambience. I hope you don't get the wrong idea about what my intentions are here. I brought you to my home because it made better sense. I bet you Mike is looking for me as I speak, wanting to discuss what vegetable side dishes to serve. If my staff could have it their way, they would own their own set of keys to my apartment."

I chuckled to myself as my nerves began to subside. "I totally see why you decided to come here. Don't worry about me thinking that you're trying to take advantage of me or something. I know you didn't plan for any of this. It's not like you picked me up and suggested to take me to your house first thing. It's just the way things happened to turn out."

"It's the way things happened to turn out, but it's not what I had in mind. Do you think you can give me a second chance at another date? Maybe we'll have our appetites back by then." He winked and flaunted a mischievous grin. His demanding eyes sought for mine and were gratified.

"Of course. I would love to." The nerves I had so skillfully tamed only seconds ago broke free from their cage and were flying around the room. My heart raced wildly while I felt my dwindling confidence slowly unravel. An object hanging on the wall proved to be my only saving grace.

"Are you a religious person?" I asked, pointing to the cross.

His enlarged pupils broke from my face to follow my outstretched finger. He studied the wall for a meditative second and shook his head. "No. No, I'm not. I don't believe in a god. But I'm not rejecting the existence of one either. I guess you can say I'm still searching for the truth. Maybe even a little forgiveness, too." His gaze became sorrowful and slowly drifted to the floor. The room fell quiet as the unexpected inquiry cracked his barricade of supremacy. The fractured wall was quickly repaired. "But enough about me for the moment. What's troubling you? Please let it out so I can show you it won't disturb our relationship."

"I was afraid we would come to this part of the night," I groaned.

"Look, if it will make you feel any better, I'll close my eyes while you tell me. Pretend I'm not sitting here, and it's just you and my noisy refrigerator. I can't see a single thing right now."

He gave me another wink and shut his eyes tight. I laughed at his scrunched expression. He held out his hands as if he knew I was staring and blindly reached for mine.

"Trust me," he whispered.

I grasped his outstretched hands and closed my eyes, too.

"I'm in a relationship right now, Marcus. I'm engaged."

His hands squeezed tighter.

"I'm engaged, but I won't be for long. I was planning to break things off before we had our first date. Things are so bad with my fiancé that he doesn't answer my phone calls anymore. I wasn't planning—"

"Shhh . . ." he whispered, placing his index finger across both my lips. "I don't need to hear anymore. Look! I'm still here."

I slowly opened my eyes and found his face was smiling. His eyes lovingly took in mine.

"You aren't disappointed?"

"Why would I be disappointed? It's not like we're in a relationship, and you've been cheating on me or something. This is how I met you. And it wasn't until last night that we really expressed what we felt for one another. So, why would your honesty offend me? Don't you know what attracts me to you?"

I shook my head.

"It's your purity. Something so precious, yet so commonly disregarded. In a world that's morally bankrupt, you stand out like a beacon of light. Let's take your decision to tell me about your engagement, for example. You could've refrained from telling me about it simply because your relationship is almost over. You could break up with your fiancé, and I would never know the difference. But that would be lying by omission, right? Most people take the road most commonly traveled. You don't. You have something in your heart that makes you beautiful," he breathed, leaning into my face. His lips slowly parted as he looked at mine. "And I find that something irresistible. Not to mention, you are extremely attractive."

My skin broke out in gooseflesh as his hands reached for the back of my neck. He pulled me in close.

"You have a lot to teach me about honesty," he uttered, smoothing my hair away from my face. "And that something starts with me tonight." His thumbs stroked the sides of my cheeks while his eyes focused on my lips. He suddenly pulled his hands from my face and straightened to his feet. "Are you sure I can't offer you something to drink? Water?"

"No, thank you."

"Well, my throat's getting dry on me. I think I'll pour myself a glass. If you don't mind, I'll just be a minute." He fled from my presence with a near run and disappeared into the dark kitchen.

I waited for him to exit so I could exhale in relief. What a gracious response to such an off-putting confession. He was so unaffected by the news that he didn't even ask any questions. It felt so good to lay all my cards out on the table and not be judged for what they disclosed. And he even requested another date! The night would be flawless, save for one detail—his parting comment. What did he mean when he said I had something to teach him about honesty? Hasn't he been truthful with me from the beginning? I looked outside the window of his apartment and watched as the blinking stream of traffic traveled down GlenPoint Strip.

The writing on the wall didn't make sense.

The looks. The heart. The wealth. The solitude. There had to be a catch somewhere. But what would that catch be? What would a man of such prestige have to hide in a relationship? My heart quickly sank as the interpretation became known.

He had a girlfriend.

That was why he was so accepting of my checkered past. He had one, too. This whole time, I've been grasping for a fistful of oil—I never realized it was running down my arm.

My posture stiffened in my chair when his dark form suddenly reappeared from the kitchen. He crossed to the back of the room and fiddled with the light that came from the inefficient lamp. The glow from a full moon illuminated his dark apartment, where the artificial did not. He took a long drink from his glass of water and set it to one side. He then straddled the back of his chair and slid it closer to mine. My eyes avoided his face for fear of what I might see.

"Gwendolyn, I want my life to be an open book to you. You took a chance in telling me something you didn't have to. It was difficult for you to do, maybe even a little scary, but you did it nonetheless. As I said before, most people take the road most commonly traveled. Well, I'm not like most people.

I want to take this path you've chosen to take and walk it with you side by side. I want to be the man you choose for your future. And I want to be there until the end. But you need to know who I am to make that kind of a decision . . ." He paused for a second and took in a deep breath. "I have something to tell you, too."

Oh, I was right. I was right! Please let it not be a girlfriend. Please . . .

I gripped the edge of my seat and refused to breathe.

Please let it not be a girlfriend. Please let it not be a girl-friend. Please let it not be a girlfriend.

"I've known about your fiancé."

"What?" I looked up from the floor and searched his face for answers. The confession was unexpected, but it certainly wasn't bad.

How could he know about my fiancé? Why, yes, of course! Our fight at the farmer's market. He was there watching us the whole time.

"I saw you at the farmer's market, too! And you have no idea how comforting it was just knowing you were there. Ryan and I were in a fight, and I could've sworn I heard you talking in my—"

"Gwendolyn, I've known about your fiancé for a while."

I closed my mouth in mid-sentence and looked at him perplexed. His eyes were compassionate, but unmistakably certain. He pulled at the collar of his shirt.

"I've known about him before I met you."

The room became quiet while I tried to process the information he was relaying. His foot tapped nervously on the floor.

"You've known about my fiancé before you met me? How is that possible?"

His eyes scanned mine and then softened. "I'm so sorry for what I'm about to tell you. I don't think there's an easy way for me to put this, but Ryan's been seeing someone else. He's been cheating on you with a good friend of mine. Well, practically anyways. I wish things were different, but . . ."

The bottom was suddenly pulled from the downward-spiraling conversation. He reached for my hand in my lap, but I recoiled.

"Why haven't you told me about this sooner?" I glared at him with newfound disgust.

He avoided my prying eyes and turned to look out the window. His head hung to his chest, and he let out a sigh. "It's me asking you now for a bit of grace."

I folded my arms across my chest and gave him nothing in response.

"Ryan is the reason why I'm here. My presence in your life was supposed to serve only one purpose . . . to distract you from him."

"To distract me from him? Why?"

"Because if you became emotionally detached, my friend would have a greater chance of getting what she wanted."

"Getting what she wanted? You mean getting him to cheat on me? That's a pretty demented thing to do, Marcus! Besides, you and I met by chance. If I hadn't pulled off to the side of the road, I would've never run into you at the beach. Isn't that right?"

"No. I wish we met by chance, but we didn't. We met because I knew where to locate you."

"And how would you know where to locate me? Is it possible that you were spying on me? Is that it? You've been spying on me this whole time, and that's how you've known about Ryan?"

"No. I would never spy on you. I needed to find you, and I did."

"But how can you know where to find me if you weren't watching where I was? Come on, Marcus! Speak the truth! You said you wanted to take the path less commonly traveled. Or have you changed your mind?"

"I possess the ability to locate someone for up to several miles away. It's one of the many ways my communication translates on land," he muttered, not looking up.

"Your communication translates on land? Are you listening to yourself? You aren't making any sense."

I shook my head in disbelief and looked the other way. I didn't get it. What kind of a sick joke was he playing? He comes into my life and sweeps me off my feet—to dump a boatload of rubbish in my lap? How dare he take a genuine moment we were sharing and turn it into a mockery! I quickly felt the hot injection of anger push through my veins. He was lucky I wasn't getting up and walking out the door.

"This won't make any sense to you until I just come out and say it."

"Until you just come out and say what?"

The intimidating eyes that were once filled with such authority went vacant. The two black holes that beheld my angry expression slowly wandered to the floor. A great deal of agony clouded his face as if it pained him to continue.

"I was once a merman."

Silence.

I couldn't believe what I was hearing. It felt as though he swung his arm back and punched me hard in my stomach. My mouth opened to speak, but nothing came out. All I could do was stare in horror at the madman who fidgeted nervously in his chair. I dug deep within my being and finally found my voice.

"A what?! Are you joking?"

"I wish I was. But what benefit would I have to ridicule myself in your presence? Do you think I want to do this to our relationship?"

"A merman?" I asked, ignoring his question. "You mean those silly creatures in fairy-tale books that my father would read to me at bedtime?"

"Yes."

"Come on! If this is a joke, you are taking it way too far. If you haven't noticed already, I'm not laughing."

He said nothing.

"You were once a merman? Ha! If what you say is true, where's your tail?" I pointed to his legs and sneered. "Do those things change with a full moon or something?"

"No. They will never change again. But even though I walk upright, I will always remain what I am. Some things can never change." His eyes slowly filled with tears and then glossed over. He raked his hand through his sweaty hair and stared back out the window. I sat there and watched while he silently suffocated in grief.

"So, tell me about yourself, Marcus. What was life like as a merman? Did you live in a colony with other merpeople and hunt for buried treasure all day?"

Even though I beat him with my words, he didn't fight back. He pulled his feet to the edge of his chair and hugged his knees to his chest. At that moment, he looked like a scared boy who lost his mom at the grocery store.

"Life in the water was lonely," he uttered from between his knees.

I was surprised he even answered my taunt.

"My father left before I was born. My mother left when I turned eight. The last memory I have of her was when she held me in her arms and told me to try my best. She was a good mother. Better than most of my kind. She taught me everything I needed to know. How to hunt. How to defend. How to entrap. I remember the night she disappeared, I had awoken from a dream and reached for her comfort in the darkness. But she was gone. She found her opportunity to receive legs, and she took care of herself. The draw for a life at the surface always takes precedence over emotional attachment in the water. It's just the way things are. And although my story sounds harsh, I was luckier than most. Many lose their parents at an even younger age and are left to fend for themselves. My mother pushed back her future to ensure I had one. I will always be grateful to her for that." He closed his eyes in remembrance. A single tear trailed down one cheek and slipped behind the collar of his shirt. "For the remainder of my life, I lived in total solitude. It wasn't until I swam to the surface that I really experienced happiness. The world above was filled with such promise. It was where I learned to speak. It was where I learned about love. I could never grow tired of watching marriage proposals or children making sandcastles with their friends. So many times, I joined families sharing memories together and wished to be a part of them. To have someone laugh at my jokes and know their smile was for me. To hold a hand in mine. To be able to tell someone I loved them and have them love me in return. But love for me was always on the outside looking in. I would leave those families at the surface and submerge back into my life that was filled with emptiness and despair. I'd fall asleep and dream of laughter, to wake up in an ocean of deafening silence. And I'd start my day all over again, receiving only fragments of someone else's experiences and claiming them as my own. Life as a merman was in a few words . . . a never-ending nightmare." He reached for his glass of water and took a small sip.

I scrutinized his face for honesty and shook my head. He was either a lunatic, a really good liar, or he was actually telling the truth.

"So, where does Ryan play a part in all of this?"

"In one of my travels, I unknowingly swam into the waters of another mermaid. Most of my kind are fiercely territorial and will defend their region to the death. But Avangeline allowed for me to enter. And thus began the birth of a very odd relationship. We made a promise to stick together and help the one if the other got out first. I received my legs before she did. So, I needed to hold up to my end of the bargain."

He suddenly stood from his curled position in his chair and crossed to the side of the room. The only thing that was visible was his long shadow gliding slowly across the floor. He walked a few creaking semi-circles and stopped.

"Life at the surface isn't a decision that can be made. It's something you have to be chosen to receive. What our kind lack that humans possess isn't legs. It's a soul. The very thing that makes you, you, that I can't stop staring at. We need someone to willingly give us that. And love is the only vehicle in which that transaction can take place. You would think it would be an easy thing for us to achieve since we are built to attract you. This hair. This face. This body. All of my features are streamlined to attract a human female. So, getting noticed really isn't the problem. It's getting love to be reciprocated that's the problem. The subject is foreign to my kind. We fumble with our words and try to imitate what we see at the surface, but it's all just a show. A mere reproduction of someone else's emotions. And although some perform well and get out fairly quickly, most are bound for a lifetime of failure. All of this needs to be done while hiding the fact that we have a tail from the waist down. Although some humans don't care if we have one or not. Or at least that's what I hear." He started pacing again. "If that rare moment occurs and love is evoked, you give them a kiss, and you are set free."

"So, this all boils down to someone giving you a kiss?"

His condescending snicker sent a shiver down my spine.

"No. If it were that easy, we'd be kissing every drunk fisherman lost at sea. It's not a kiss that gives us legs. It's what transpires during the kiss. It's what the action represents. When love is truly given away, a kiss is the only portal through which the soul is released."

"And what happens to the person once they've released their soul?"

He stopped pacing in his semi-circle to look at the cross on the wall. The rapid adjustment in his breathing could be heard from across the room.

"They become nothing. They dry up and crumble into nothing. My victim fell to the floor and vanished right before my very eyes. Her body became as the sand and washed away with the next wave, never to be seen again. And at that moment, I felt my first real human emotion. And do you know what that emotion was? Shame. I just killed someone to receive a life of my own, and all I could feel was shame. Nobody ever prepared me for that. I exited the shore with legs that took years to acquire and never wanted to look back. But even now, as I close my eyes, I can't get her face out of my head. My life changed when I became a human, Gwendolyn. I have a place of my own now. I have a nice car. I own a club. I have a wealth of resources at the ocean's floor to give me all the money I need. But nothing can take away my past. It doesn't matter how hard I scrub with soap; it doesn't wash away in the shower. My scarlet stain will always remain." He looked down at his outstretched hands and turned them over to reveal his palms. "If this skin tears, you will see scales beneath. It's an ever-present reminder of who I really am."

The day he saved me on the rocks! His back! I wasn't hallucinating?

"To answer your question about Ryan, he's fallen in love with Avangeline. She's quite certain of that. She truly feels it will take only one more encounter, and she will get what she needs. I held up to my end of the bargain and distracted you from him. And before I knew who you were, I didn't care about the logistics of your relationship. But after I met you and saw what a beautiful creature he was throwing away, I became convinced he doesn't deserve your affection. I can give you what he fails to provide. I can give you fidelity."

I avoided his eyes and remained quiet. He waited for me to respond and then continued.

"I could never understand the purpose of my kind. They are cruel, heartless beings, and the way they obtain legs is even crueler still. But what can be said about a being who is heartless even though they possess one?"

He stepped out from the corner of the room and sat back in his chair. The eyes that were once pained and clouded were hard and menacing. It was as if a switch was thrown, and he had become a different person.

"He doesn't love you. He doesn't, and he hasn't for a while. And, in my eyes, to throw away your love is inexcusable. I would've given anything to receive such an honor. He drinks of your adoration and throws you away like a used-up soda can. He's no different than the creatures that live in the ocean. Only, they are part animal. He is not. He's making his decisions by choice. They make their decisions by instinct. So, let me be honest with you, there's a type of satisfaction as I hear the reports from Avangeline. And if all she needs is one more visit from Ryan, I'd feel great pleasure to bring him to her myself. It's my love for you that restrains my vengeance."

"What do you mean you'd bring him to her?" I asked, pulling from my stupor. "Are you talking about dragging him to the beach against his will?" He spoke with such conviction that I actually believed what he was saying.

"I don't need to use physical force with Ryan," he said with a sneer. "I'd use common influence."

"Common influence?"

"Earlier in our conversation, you questioned my ability to locate you without spying. I mentioned it was one of the many ways my communication translates on land. There's really no use for a spoken language underwater. Our senses are the same as yours, only they are highly developed. Through a system of thoughts and impulses, we are interrelated to each other by something called common influence. You see it in a school of fish or a flock of birds. As one swims or flies in one direction, the others will follow its lead. This ability to control others' movements is used primarily for the fleeing of predators. And although we don't usually live in groups, when we are together, we're so intimately connected that we become as one organism. This is why most of my kind choose to live alone. It's hard to bend to another's will, and there's always a dominant force that drives . . ." He paused from his speaking to take another drink. He set his empty glass on the windowsill and adjusted his chair. "We also possess the ability to locate our food for up to several miles away, as do many other marine animals. So, for our living environment underwater, these hypersensitive senses served a very practical purpose. But when our bodies change for land, they remain as mere additions to the ones you possess. Only now our common influence isn't shared between mermaids, but between humans."

"Are you saying that your influence can control human movements now?"

"Yes."

"And human thoughts?"

"Yes."

"So, this whole time I've heard you speaking in my head . . . It wasn't my imagination?"

"When I speak within your mind, I speak to your soul."

My jaw dropped open, and I stared at him in astonishment. I couldn't believe what I was hearing! The voice within my head that I rationalized as a figment of my imagination was real the whole time?

"Then it was you? Using the influence? It was you who brought me to the shore those two times when we met? My attraction to the beach I never could explain. It was all you?"

"Yes."

I took in a deep breath and let it out in a sputter. My illogical decisions to visit the beach were all at once explained with the theatrics of a circus trick. At least I could comfort myself knowing I wasn't crazy. I fussed with the hem of my sweater and coughed. "Why did you do all this to me?"

He started to mutter something under his breath and then withdrew.

I covered my face with my hands and groaned. "Forget about it. So, where do I go from here? I just found out that my fiancé is cheating on me, and the man of my dreams turns out to be a merman. What am I supposed to do with my life now? Everything that I thought was, wasn't. Ryan never cared for me. And you . . . well, I don't know what to think about you anymore."

"Do you think you can still love me?" he asked simply.

I said nothing.

"You still love Ryan, then?"

Silence.

"But how can you still love him when you know the truth about what he's doing? Do you doubt what I say? Test me! Give him a chance to show his true intentions. If he's a man of his word, the beach will pose no threat to your relationship. Take him there. Do it in a way where he can slip away and not be noticed if he chooses to do so. Invite a few people. Or, better yet, invite many. If he loves you, and I am nothing but a liar, he will remain by your side. And you will have a greater confidence in someone who is highly questionable. But know this—I speak the truth. If you choose to marry Ryan, you will unite with a man who has given his heart to someone else. He may not consummate his love with Avangeline. But if the intentions are there, he will do so with another. "

"And how can you be so certain he will give his soul away with one more encounter? What if it takes several?" I asked in repulsion. I bent at my waist and winced as I was suddenly feeling sick.

"Are you feeling okay?"

"I'm fine," I lied, straightening in my chair.

"Avangeline mentioned she was going to prove her love with a gift. I gave one to my victim, and she thinks that's why I was so successful in getting out quickly."

"What was the gift you gave to your victim?"

"A pearl necklace."

"A pearl necklace?"

"Yeah. Just something I put together with some fishing line and a handful of pearls."

A pearl necklace.

The room started to spin. The white walls blended into the dim lamp, which blended into the dark figure in the chair. I hung my head between my knees as a cold sweat broke out over my body. I felt like I was going to faint.

Emma. He killed Emma.

"Emma," I groaned, clutching my stomach in nausea. "Emma."

"What?"

"Emma. You killed Emma." I mustered all the strength I could and propped myself up in my chair. His tense face looked at mine and paled to gray.

"You killed Emma. Didn't you?"

His fingers trembled slightly as he covered his mouth with his hand.

"Emma was your victim. Wasn't she? Wasn't she?!"

"But how could you know about Em . . . Em . . . Emma? Was she your . . . your . . ."

"My best friend who's missing? The person my father spoke of, who the police presume is dead? Yes!"

Before I knew what I was doing, I rose to my feet and slapped him hard across his cheek. I slapped him so hard my hand stung with fire.

"You killed her! Didn't you? Didn't you?!"

He flinched from my hand as I struck him again and again. His face swelled instantly from the repetitive blows.

"How could you do this to me? You . . . you . . . monster!"

I dropped my throbbing hand to my side and looked around his apartment in panic. I needed to get out. If he could do something so unspeakable to her, he could do something so unspeakable to me. I grabbed my purse from the floor and ran for the door.

"Wait! Gwendolyn, please! I didn't know she was your friend! Please! I would never want to—"

I threw open his door and stumbled out into the hall. Before I reached the staircase, a yell of agony sounded from his apartment.

Chapter Eleven

ll I could do was run.

Storefronts passed by in a blur. Crowds scattered from mingling. A police officer glared in speculation. I didn't care. I tore down the sidewalk of GlenPoint Strip as if the devil himself was nipping at my heels. I bumped into a child carrying an ice cream cone, and she dropped it. Her tiny scream rose from the throng of people circulating behind me. I turned to observe my trespass, but I didn't stop. I couldn't. Every time I slowed in speed, the truth was there, waiting for my acknowledgment. A group of men circling in front of a liquor store dispersed and catcalled something vulgar. I accelerated upon hearing their remark and slammed hard into a man wearing a black leather jacket. He staggered to one side and yelled for me to slow down. I heeded his request as my legs suddenly seized from exhaustion. I needed to stop just long enough to catch my breath. My hands clutched the sides of my stomach while a sharp cramp pierced into one side. I entered a poorly lit section of the street and stumbled on a restaurant's decorative planter. I lost my footing and fell hard to the pavement.

A breath. All I needed was a breath.

I curled in fetal position and took several burning gasps. A loud laugh broadcasted across the sidewalk. A younger couple gawked at the spectacle. I groaned loudly as I rolled to my stomach and lifted my body to my knees. I took in a fiery breath and held it.

"Just something I put together with some fishing line and a handful of pearls."

I pushed my hands against my ears and let out a cry in anguish. An older man walking his dog down the street stopped and turned in concern.

"Hello, miss? Are you feeling okay?"

I looked down at myself and blushed in embarrassment. Tousled hair, panting, crouched on all fours—I looked no different than his shaggy companion slobbering on a leash.

"Miss?"

"Yes, I'm fine. Thank you," I grunted, lifting to my feet. I turned over my hands and wiped off a cigarette butt that was smashed into one palm. I brushed away the gravel that clung to my clothes and pulled my sweater over my exposed waist. "I was running, and I didn't see where I was going. I tripped and fell on that planter over there." I looked around at my surroundings and for the first time noticed where I was. Surprisingly, I had run all but three blocks from my house. I made better time than I thought.

"I just need to get back home."

"Well, if you're sure you're okay . . ."

"But how could you know about Em . . . Em . . . Emma?"

I whipped my head to one side and winced in repulsion. "Yes. I'm sure I'll be fine. But I really must be on my way."

I thanked him for his concern and started in the direction of my house. I paced myself to a jog while I sifted through the rubble in my brain. I needed to think. If I could take a hot shower and slip into some comfortable pajamas, I could think through my problems and possibly find some answers. Or I could just pull the covers over my head and pretend I was dead. My parents were my biggest obstacle at this point. They would be awaiting my arrival. And they would want to know how my date went with Marcus. Perhaps a quick explanation of feeling sick would sweep all the gritty details under the rug. I pulled my cell phone from my purse and turned it on.

Nine thirty-three.

I grumbled in displeasure and slipped it back inside. Not only were my parents awake, but they would question why my date ended so early. And unless I was willing to explain the last forty-five minutes of torture, a lie would definitely be in order. The problem was that they were professionals when it came to lies. They could smell them. My facial expressions, my cracking voice, my body language—all were calculated responses to their probing questions.

For the remainder of my jog home, I remained completely occupied with my parents' dreaded confrontation.

I pulled open the front door and took several steps down the hall. My mother was seated on the couch, draped in a blanket, reading a magazine. She turned at the sound of the door closing and looked at me in surprise.

"Oh, honey! You're home? I didn't hear Marcus pull in."

"Hey, Mom." I forced an artificial smile. I stopped before I entered the living room and inched my way closer to the staircase. I didn't want her to question my dirty clothes. "Our date ended a little early."

"Why?" she asked, her eyes widening in alarm. She folded her magazine across her lap to give me her full attention. Her eyes scanned my face and then dropped to a gray smudge of dirt that marked the front of my sweater. I found the shadiest part of the hallway and hugged it. I was suddenly feeling sick.

"Did everything go okay? You look like you're not feeling very well."

"That's because I just experienced the worst night of my life," I stated with sincerity. "I was sick to my stomach the entire time we were together. We never ate at a restaurant or watched a movie. We just sat and talked. But even that was nauseating. I came home early so I could get some relief. I've needed to throw up ever since I sat in his car." I hated lying to my parents, but the situation left me no choice. My eyes focused on the sofa where she sat.

"Oh, sweetheart! I'm sorry. Do you think you caught the flu? There's always a terrible bug going around this time of year."

I looked up at her innocent inquiry and tried my best to smile. I would give anything for it to be the flu. "I don't know, Mom. But I wouldn't worry about it. I'm sure my nerves and the excitement of my first date got the best of me. I just want to go upstairs and take a hot shower."

"Well, I was just going to suggest that you do that. I'll bring up your robe and a fresh pair of pajamas. I washed a load of your clothes, and they're drying in the dryer right now."

I leaned against the wall and winced in discomfort. It was like my stomach had grown teeth and was chewing on the inside of my throat. My mother noticed my look of unease and stood in alarm.

"Warm pajamas sound great. I'm sorry I can't stay and talk. But I really don't feel well."

"I understand completely, honey. You go on up and get some rest," she said, shooing me with her hands. "I'll be up in a little while to see how you're doing."

"Thanks," I called over my shoulder. The knots in my neck unraveled as I made my way up the staircase. My excuse worked. And the fact that I was legitimately sick only helped in its plausibility.

"Oh, sweetheart?"

"Yes?"

"Before I forget to tell you, Ryan called tonight. I told him you were out, but I didn't give him any explanations. I figured it wasn't my place to say anything."

"Ryan called?" I shuddered at the mention of his name.

"To answer your question about Ryan, he's fallen in love with Avangeline. She's quite certain of that. She truly feels it will take only one more encounter, and she will get what she needs."

"Yes, dear. He called at about eight-thirty or so."

I clasped my hand over my mouth as a familiar burning liquid suddenly flooded the back of my throat. I lunged forward and ascended the stairs two at a time.

"Dear, are you okay? Dear?"

I barely made it to the toilet before I emptied the contents of my stomach.

I turned on the lamp at my bedside and pulled my covers to my chin. The hot shower felt good. After several attempts at throwing up and eliminating nothing more than bile, a thorough cleansing was well appreciated. My mother brought up my pajamas, still warm from the dryer. By the time I brushed my teeth and curled up in my favorite blanket, I felt like I was ready to conquer the world. When life felt as though it was spinning on its head, I wanted nothing more than to sleep my worries away. Only this time, a bed of cozy fleece wasn't going to solve my problems. And I knew what I needed to do. I reached into my nightstand and pulled out the red leather journal my parents gave me for my birthday. I thumbed to the back page and retrieved the formal business card that was tucked away in its cover. The bold lettering burrowed deep into my eyes until I could see it when I blinked.

Officer Black ext. 356

He told us to call him as soon as we discovered any information pertaining to Emma's disappearance. And I didn't only have information, I had the name of her killer. By his own admission or lack of denial, Marcus murdered Emma in cold blood. So many sleepless nights of questions and concerns could finally be answered with one simple name. And what would Officer Black think of his ridiculous story? Mermaids obtaining legs by stealing people's souls? He would question his sanity for sure. Whether it was a prison, an insane asylum, or a scientist's laboratory—Marcus would disappear in some form of institution. And I would never see him again.

But was his story real?

Was the account that sounded as though it was stolen from a child's fairy-tale book true? I couldn't deny the fact that I saw fish scales under his torn skin. And the countless times I heard his voice talking in my head did turn out to be genuine. He did it for me on the spot! If he was telling the truth, then his remorse for killing Emma was probably legitimate as well. And I was witness to that. He wasn't only regretful about his past—he was tormented. Should a man who committed a crime in ignorance be punished for life? Surely, that was not my place to decide. I had a responsibility to report what I discovered, and there was nothing more to consider.

I rested my head against my pillow and hooked my hands behind my head.

And what did I feel for Ryan?

He was my first love and my fiancé, but was he unfaithful? Or was I so wrapped up in the mystery of Emma that I chose to neglect our relationship? Was his sudden withdrawal in some way my fault? My mind flooded back to the wonderful memories we shared over the past few years. I would've never imagined our love would come to an end. And I would've never imagined myself with another man. I was so enraptured with Marcus's mystical charm that I failed to notice how uncomfortable I was with him. I was either struggling to retain my confidence, or I was bursting at the seams with desire. I didn't love Marcus. I was in lust with Marcus. When Ryan and I were together, I could be myself with no restrictions. There was no grappling for words or feelings of insecurity because I was with my best friend. He had his faults, some that needed to be dealt with immediately, but he was my true love nonetheless. And I needed to look deep into his heart if I was going to consider him for my future. I couldn't throw away our love for a few weeks of disorder. He deserved another chance.

Suddenly, as if my unspoken request was granted, a loud buzzing sounded from my purse. I didn't have to look at my cell phone to know who it was.

"Hey, Ryan! How are you?"

"Gwen? Hey . . . where've you been? I've been trying to call you back all night."

"You've been trying to call me back?"

"Yeah. You called and said you had something really important to tell me. I would've responded sooner, but I was having a serious conversation with my dad."

"Oh, right. I did call earlier." With all that transpired in the night, I forgot I called to break things off. So much has changed since that phone call before my date. And so many questions were raised that needed to be asked. Only, they were questions that couldn't be asked with words, but with actions.

"If he is a man of his word, the beach will pose no threat to your relationship. Take him there! Do it in a way where he can slip away and not be noticed if he chooses to do so. Invite a few people, or better yet, invite many."

"Well, I was calling because I had a great idea. How does a party at the beach sound? I thought we could throw one in celebration of our engagement. I know it's a little late for announcements, but—"

"A party? You want to celebrate our engagement?" he questioned, cutting me short. "Are you serious?"

I could picture the look on his face as he began to laugh. His lack of enthusiasm for my idea hurt.

"Sure, I'm serious. Why wouldn't I be? I want to share the good news with our friends. Did you even tell Joey you proposed?"

"Of course, I told Joey I proposed! I didn't know you cared so much about my friends. And what kind of party would it be anyways? Don't you remember how our last little gathering turned out?"

"Yes, I remember," I grumbled under my breath. The last party we attended was with Emma. His friends sat around a smoking bonfire all night, telling dirty jokes and burping. His interest in the subject was going to be dead if I didn't come up with a solution. My response needed to make sense. "It lacked excitement because there weren't any pretty girls to liven up the atmosphere. But I can solve that problem really quickly. I can invite Jessica."

The line was quiet.

"You know, the girl from Officer Black's meeting? I'm sure I can convince her to invite a few of her friends. And they, of course, will invite their friends. Before we know it, the guys will be reciting poetry by firelight under the stars. They'll be stoked to come. Don't you think?"

"Well, yeah. But you don't even like Jessica. I don't get it, Gwen. What's this all about? All of my friends already know about our engagement. And your friends . . . well, you're going to invite people you don't even know?"

"I want to turn over a new leaf in our relationship. I know we haven't been getting along lately, and I take the blame for some of that. I want to change a lot of things about myself. You told me once that I never talked about our engagement. Well, this is my way of trying to start over. I want to give our relationship another chance."

"But you don't have to do it by throwing a party. Just telling me you want to start over is enough for me. It's more than you've given in weeks."

The ache in his voice cut me to the heart. I didn't need to see proof that he was faithful. My confidence would come with time, healing, and effort. The more I invested in our relationship, the more I would receive. My party at the beach would only introduce more suspicion. And he would be hurt if he knew the real motive behind it.

"But . . . I guess it does sound kinda fun. And you are right about one thing—the guys will jump at the chance to meet a group of hot, available chicks. Just make sure they are to be sure. The night will be a colossal waste of time if they aren't interesting. What time were you thinking of having it?"

I was trapped! It was too late to backtrack.

"Uh . . . how does this Friday sound? I can make out some quick invitations to make it official."

"Friday sounds great. Wow, Gwen. You really surprise me sometimes. I was sure our relationship was over. In fact, I know this sounds funny and all, but I was sure you were calling tonight because you wanted to break things off. It was just a hunch, I guess. But I'm really glad I was wrong.

I've missed you, you know. I'll let the guys know first thing tomorrow."

At that moment, I felt no bigger than three inches tall. He wasn't the creep in the relationship. I was.

"That sounds great, Ryan. We can figure out all the details later. And, hey . . ."

"Yeah?"

"I love you."

"I love you, too."

I hung up and reached for my journal on my nightstand. I never considered myself to be a murderer. But I was fairly certain Ryan wouldn't let me down. I would call Officer Black after I proved Marcus's story was wrong. That is, if Ryan is honest. My doubts began to creep in as I wrote the invitations.

***

Thick smoke nearly choked me as I pushed my way through the crowded entrance. La Mer, the brick building that was vacant when I visited, was packed with guests. I blinked and waited as my eyes adjusted to the hazy candlelight that flickered across the room. Many people wove their way in and out of shadows, seamlessly blending into the thick tapestries that covered the walls. A heavyset man watching me from afar grinned and lifted his glass briefly before taking a small sip. I met his eyes with a steady gaze and tried my best to smile. It was a weak attempt, and I was suddenly thankful for the veil of darkness that hid my quivering lips. I purposed within my heart that my decision was final and willed my stubborn body to move forward.

I cautiously stepped out from the doorway's safeguard and into the mysterious club, where I began my search. I examined the couples that were seated at the bar, followed by the bustle of people on the dance floor. I noticed a few tables tucked away in the corner of the room, inviting those who sought privacy.

Perhaps he was there.

The bottom of my stomach suddenly dropped as a strong wave of nausea took over. I clasped my hand over my mouth and instinctively looked for the nearest restroom. I was mortified at the thought of throwing up in front of people. I was even more mortified at what I was doing.

"Miss, do you have any identification?"

Snapping back into reality, I focused on a short man with black hair and narrowed eyes. They looked me over in appreciation.

"Who, me?"

"Yes, you. Are you twenty-one? I don't see your wristband." He craned his neck to get a better look at my arm.

The pulse from the bass of the music filled my head, throbbing a rhythm that repeated itself over and over. My mind scrambled for an excuse, but instead rebelled and drained of all thought. I stood there for a humiliating moment, unable to speak.

"Twenty-one. Identification. Where is it?" He crossed his arms across his chest and waited for an answer. The expression that was once explorative began to look annoyed.

I bit my lower lip and looked the other way. During the countless times I imagined this night, I never once thought to show proof of my age. I needed to buy myself some time and come up with a plausible excuse for not having any. I unzipped the flap of my purse and clumsily sifted through its contents.

"I could've sworn it was here," I stammered, trying to spill some of my cosmetics onto the floor. I slowly knelt to one knee and retrieved a lipstick that rolled under a chair. "I remember putting my driver's license in my wallet, but I can't find it for some reason. Did I put it here in this side pocket? No. Maybe it's in my jeans?" I turned my face and winced at my inadequate skill at lying. The bouncer's scowl showed he wasn't buying any of it either. I needed to be truthful about my intentions if I planned to go any further.

"Look, sir, let me be honest with you. I came here to tell someone something really important. I'll leave right after I meet with him, and you'll never see me again. You can watch me if you don't believe what I'm saying. But I assure you, I have no other motive. Please give me one minute to find him." A cold sweat collected at the back of my neck and slowly dripped down the front of my shirt.

His hardened face studied mine as he considered my simple request. For a split second, I thought he would agree. He walked the length of a table and stroked his angular jaw. His quick stride suddenly came to a halt, and he shook his head.

"No. I'm sorry. I've heard that one a hundred times before. If I say yes, you'll disappear in the crowd, and I'll have a drunk minor on my hands. This is why people carry cell phones. If you needed to contact this person that badly, you should've tried calling the front desk. But now I'm going to ask for you to leave. And if it weren't for your lying earlier, I would've trusted you enough to walk yourself to the door. I think it's best if I escort you the whole way there. And please don't try to run. It will only make matters worse." He took a step forward, appearing to brace himself for a rebellious response.

I willingly submitted to the small attendant, who seized me by my upper arm and parted his way through a nearby crowd. Several onlookers smirked in our direction as he bellowed loudly for oblivious dancers to clear from our path. An unaware couple immersed in a conversation halted our progression forward.

"Don't worry about this one, Jake. I'll take it from here."

The security guard's body stiffened. He dropped my arm like a venomous snake and turned around to obey his command.

Marcus was seated within a few feet from where we stood and was watching the whole spectacle. With a simple snap of his fingers, his authoritative presence was all at once made known. The shrew-like bouncer bowed with an apology and scurried away to a dark corner of the room. The two women who were draped across Marcus's chest craned their necks in curiosity and smiled.

I struggled to focus on the shadowed trio, but the room began to spin. My stomach pitched and rolled. I fell forward and gripped the edge of the table to steady myself.

"Already wanting to leave? You just got here, didn't you?" His voice was thick. He uttered a deep chuckle, and the two women began giggling along, both visibly intoxicated.

I straightened my composure in an effort to appear brave. My hand fumbled in my pants pocket and pulled out its contents. "I have something for you," I said bluntly, feeling a fleeting measure of courage. I pushed the folded invitation across the table.

He released his hold from the brunette's waist and reached for the singular piece of paper. His hand slowly closed around it, making a tight fist. "That's it?" he asked, raising one eyebrow. His face suddenly darkened, showing a mixture of anger and hurt. "No hello? No thoughts on how I've been?"

I studied his face. His eyes held mine, and for a brief moment, my heart lurched with a familiar longing. He was magnificent tonight. His wide, defined chest was embraced by one woman while the other stroked his wavy black hair. A muscle in his jaw tightened.

"How have you been these past few days?" His voice quivered slightly, catching me off guard.

I looked down, somewhat stunned at his visible show of concern. The two women who ignored my presence until now muttered something about my face and laughed. I looked up to find him still staring. His eyes were two black pools—deep, steady, and tranquil.

I'm falling in them.

"I planned a party at the beach," I whispered. "You can let your friend know Ryan will be there. If you'll excuse me now, I'll be on my way."

As my parting words were spoken, the curtains were drawn on his raw, exposed emotions. His once lack of interest in the women became alive, almost robotic. One of them squealed while he nuzzled his face into the side of her neck. They were excited, like two puppies begging for any show of affection.

"I'll let her know," he uttered under the silky blanket of hair.

"Come back when you're old enough to get a license," one of the females snarled. The other broke her lusting embrace long enough to give a high-pitched laugh. I shuddered at the ignorance of their grievous plight and turned to walk away.

I couldn't move.

I stifled a scream that filled my throat as I began to panic. The fast beat of music, the drone of many voices, the two women pathetically squealing for attention—all faded to silence. The only sound I heard was the thundering of my heart pounding in my ears. My mind repeatedly told my feet to run, but they were locked in place, refusing to comply.

And then, as simply as one moving a chess piece across a game board, his eyes slowly turned my unwilling body around. I balled my hands in tight fists and shut my eyes in terror.

There I stood before him. My eyes remained closed, for I knew if I opened them, I would undoubtedly bend to his will. A small bead of sweat trickled down my cheek and ran into the corner of my mouth.

"Marcus, please . . ." I begged in my mind.

He gave a brief allowance for movement as though my request struck some unseen chord.

"Please let me go. You want me to be with you willingly, not by force."

My limbs felt swollen and heavy. My mouth was thick and dry. His companions crackled with enthusiastic chatter as they questioned my perplexing hesitation.

"I did what you suggested. See, the invitation is proof that I believe you. Only please let me go . . ."

Time before him felt like an eternity. Someone bumped into the side of my arm and apologized. As badly as I wanted to open my eyes to see what was happening, I knew I couldn't.

"Please . . ."

The numerous pleas, as trite as they sounded, moved the monster's pity. The strong grip of power that held my body in paralysis slowly released. At first, my movement took effort as if my legs were encased in cement. And then, as a bird being released from a snare, I burst through the dining area in search of an exit.

I stumbled out of the door of the club feeling as though I was being sucked through a nightmare. My breaths came in short gasps while I struggled for the sea air to fill my thirsty lungs. My back was soaked with perspiration, causing my shirt to cling to my skin. I unclenched my stinging fists and looked down to see dark maroon crescents—blood markings from my nails digging deep into my palms.

I have Ryan's blood on my hands.

I gave a sharp cry and wiped them down the front of my jeans. People walked by me in a blur as I traveled down the crowded sidewalk of GlenPoint. I broke through a small group of couples lingering around the front entrance of the club and for the first time noticed how severely underdressed I was. I looked down at my jeans streaked brown with blood and scuffed ballet flats. My white t-shirt clung to my damp skin, undoubtedly revealing the pink polka-dotted bra I mistakenly chose to wear. I must have stuck out like a sore thumb!

I entered the large parking lot at the end of the street and spotted my car softly glowing under a burnt-out street lamp.

Its presence was strangely comforting, like seeing a long-lost friend on the first day of school. I leaned against the cold, heavy door and allowed for my weight to slowly release. My composure was holding together by threads.

How does one sear a conscience?

I tilted my head back and took in a silent, starless sky. There were no answers to my question.

***

"Marcus! Where are you going? You're not leaving our company so soon, are you?"

I shook away the annoying woman who clung to my side and quickly stood to my feet. A loud thud sounded from the floor as a mass of satin and curls fell off the booth. Ashlyn reached for her friend's hand to pull her up, but only dragged her to a flattened position on the seat. One of them burped loudly, and they both began to laugh.

"You're drunk, Ashlyn. You both are. I'm going to call a cab to take you two home. In fact, I think I'll do that right now." I looked down at Melissa shamelessly lying in the booth and shook my head in repulsion. You take a woman who had a small measure of decency and give her a few drinks—she winds up sprawled out in public with her dress around her neck. I couldn't understand why humans drank a toxic liquid to act so foolishly. Such a lack of self-control was a turn-off.

"But didn't you want to hang out with us tonight? We thought you wanted to have a good time," Ashlyn slurred, propping herself up on both elbows.

"Yes, I said I wanted to have a good time. But now I think that time is up."

"Huh?"

They didn't understand my intentions, and I didn't expect them to. I was only using them for their appearance. When Gwendolyn called the front desk and said she was dropping off something for me, I thought a couple of women would be the perfect foil. I was hoping she would feel jealous and want me back. Unfortunately, she was probably disgusted with my behavior and thought I had solicited the women of the night. It was a bad idea from the start.

"Meet me at the front of the club, ladies. If you will excuse me, I have a phone call to make."

I stepped over Ashlyn, who was still lying on the floor, and disappeared into the crowd.

Chapter Twelve

For the past forty-five minutes, my face remained stuck in a permanent, phony smile. Every once in a while, I gave a nod and the occasional 'uh-huh'. But for the majority of the time, I stayed silent as Jessica maintained a one-way conversation she was having with herself. My expression was so forced that the muscles in my cheeks were beginning to hurt.

". . . and then I just told him off. And do you know what his response was? He was like, well, I was going to leave you anyways. And I was like, yeah right! You just bought me an expensive handbag two hours ago. Can you believe what he was saying? He tried to say he was going to break up with me first. The nerve of that filthy dog!" She reached behind her back and retied her sparkly halter top that slipped to her bra. I looked down at my sherbet-colored sundress and smoothed down the ruffles that were fluttering in the wind.

She gave a loud groan and continued her rant. "I'm looking at this guy and thinking . . . I can't have a relationship with someone I can't kiss. Just the thought of getting close to his mouth makes me want to vomit. But I guess I put up with a lot because his daddy makes six figures. It's the price you pay for materialism, right? Oh, never mind. You don't understand what I'm talking about. You're actually in a relationship for love. I just don't know how you guys do it," she finished, shaking her head in bewilderment. She took a small sip from her soda can and waited for me to respond.

"Uh-huh."

"No really, Gwen. How?"

"What?" I didn't recognize a question had been asked.

"How do you and Ryan do it? I mean, you guys have been together for forever now. I can't even hold a relationship with my dog for that long!"

I gazed at her oversized sunglasses, stunned that she asked me a question. It was a miracle! The egocentric clouds have parted, and a small ray of consideration was finally shining through. She really wanted to hear what I had to say?

"Well, I'm not sure," I reflected, sweeping my hair behind my shoulders. "I think it's important to find someone who shares your interests. Someone who isn't just good-looking, but has a great personality as well. You have to find the whole package if you want to make it work." I looked across the sand at Ryan, who was grabbing a drink from the cooler. He threw one to Joey, who burped loudly and smashed an empty can on his forehead. The four friends began grunting wildly in an outward display of fabricated manhood. Suddenly, as if he felt my curious stare, Ryan turned in the direction where I was standing and smiled. My eyes pleaded with his as Jessica began to speak again.

"But the whole package is so hard to find! For instance, I was shopping at the mall one time and met this really hot guy at the food court. He offered to buy me lunch, and of course, I accepted because he was at least five years older than me. His hand brushed against mine, and it felt really rough. Like sandpaper, you know? I figured he had a job that used his hands. Like a construction worker, or a mechanic, or something. And that would make sense because his body was so built. Anyways, what was I talking about? Oh right, the perfect package . . ."

"Excuse me, Jessica," Ryan interrupted, circling his arms around my waist. "But I think I have the answer to all your life's problems. You were talking about finding the perfect package, right?"

"Right . . ." she answered, taking another sip.

"Well, you're in luck because your perfect package just happens to be here today! And he shares all the same qualities you do. He wears knee-high leather boots. He has tattoos that hold no significance, and he wears way too much hairspray."

She peered over the rim of her sunglasses and rolled her eyes. I couldn't help but laugh at her irritation.

"And who might that be, cupid?"

"Just look across the blanket and behold your future boyfriend. He's the handsome gentleman sporting red and blue braids."

Jessica squinted in the direction of where Joey was seated and gave a slight frown. "Joey Monroe?"

"Yes, Joey Monroe. And don't let his bad-boy exterior fool you. Underneath that leather jacket adorned with chains and studs stands a man who's as cuddly as a teddy bear. He can let himself go at a party. And he can let himself go as a man . . . if you know what I mean."

"Ryan!" I corrected, barely audible above his explosion of laughter. "This isn't some dating game you're hosting. Let the two meet at their own pace."

"He has a tattoo?" Jessica asked, raising one eyebrow.

"Yes, he does. And believe me, he has more than one. Hey, Joey!"

"Yeah?"

"How many tattoos are you sporting now these days, man? Seven?"

"Only five, bro. Why?"

"You have five tattoos?" Jessica asked, stepping out from our circle.

Joey's face clouded with confusion as he processed the unexpected questioner. He then glanced at Ryan, who was smiling from ear to ear. He motioned for his puzzled friend to join our conversation.

"Yes, I have five," he answered, stepping in closer.

"Really? Well, five just happens to be my lucky number. What tattoos do you have?" Jessica asked, flashing a flirtatious smile. She flipped her hair to one shoulder.

Joey's face filled with pride when he detected her growing level of interest. He pulled back his shoulders and pushed out his chest like a young rooster strutting arrogantly in a hen house. "I have a snake that coils around my left ankle.

A pair of dice here, on my wrist. Two stars on both shoulder blades, and a dagger that's thrust in my back."

"The dagger is thrust in your back?"

"Well, yeah. Or it's supposed to look that way. The handle is coming out with a small trickle of blood running down one side. I got it to symbolize all the people that hurt me over the years."

"Oh, right! I get it. They all hurt you because they stabbed you in the back. How poetic. What a coincidence you have five tattoos because I have five of them myself."

"Really? Well, what are they, and where are they?" he asked, crossing his arms across his chest. His upper lip curled slightly as he unashamedly checked her out.

"I have a fairy here, on my ankle. A bat on my upper thigh. My name is written on the back of my neck, and angel wings are on my shoulder blades."

"Angel wings? Sss . . ." Joey hissed and shook his hand like he touched something hot. "Either it's getting hotter out here, or I think I just found my soulmate. Jessica, baby, where have you been all my life?"

She gave his arm a playful push and let out a high-pitched squeal. "Oh, Joey. You're so funny. I'm surprised we haven't met sooner. We really do have a lot in common, don't we? Come and tell me where you got all those interesting tattoos. I want to know the story behind every one." She knelt on the ground to gather her belongings and said something to a friend sitting nearby. She then hooked her arm around his shoulder and led him to the furthest end of the lifeguard station.

Ryan and I stood in silence as we watched the newly established couple walk across the sand and disappear behind a hill. The snickering and jokes we exchanged were quickly replaced with shock.

"What the heck just happened?" Ryan asked, looking at me baffled. "I suggested for Jessica to notice Joey, but I never thought she would actually be interested! Either I'm going crazy, or my best friend just hooked up with a chick."

"Nope. You're not going crazy. He just hooked up with a chick. But not without the help from his trusty sidekick. Now, what are you going to do about the rest of the crowd?"

We scanned the flapping blanket of guests and took in a party that showed no signs of coexisting. Bryan and Dallas were seated in front of the cooler, immersed in a heated debate over what video games sucked more. Alice, Lindsay, and Ayesha were clustered at the opposite end of the blanket, whispering something rumored about someone they disliked. One side was totally oblivious that the other even existed.

"What happened to this party?" he asked, plopping down onto the sand. "It's like somebody cut the blanket in half and separated the two pieces by gender. If I knew it was going to be this boring, I would've suggested for everyone to bring their bathing suits. But you have to hand it to Jessica for delivering what she promised—single females who are halfway decent looking. It's no wonder the guys are talking about video games . . . they're too intimidated to make their move. It looks like I'll have to play matchmaker all night." He reached up to grab me around my waist and pulled me into his lap. His long arms encircled my legs as I drew them to my chest.

"Oh, come on now. Let the guys take care of themselves. You and I need to spend some time together and talk. We haven't had a quiet moment with each other all day." The party had started nearly three hours ago, yet we shared only a handful of words in passing. Either he was having a conversation with one of his friends, or I was trapped by Jessica's inconsiderate jabbering. We talked more in the car ride over than in all of our encounters at the party combined.

"Well, here's our moment then," he whispered, cuddling into the back of my neck. "It doesn't get any quieter than this."

"Right," I muttered. I stared at the muscle that pulled in his arm as he softly caressed the side of one knee. "I'm glad we're finally alone because I really need to talk to you about something. It has to do with our relationship and the past couple of months."

"The last couple of months?" His hold grew abruptly stiff.

"Yes. I think we need to talk about the problems we've been experiencing and what we can do to fix them. Our relationship has been confusing for me, Ryan. One minute we're doing great and getting married. The next minute, we're fighting like cats and dogs and are hardly speaking to each other. We've changed so much in the past few weeks that it feels like we're living in two separate worlds. I can't see myself marrying a man who has become so polar opposite of myself." I broke from his embrace to get a good look at his face. His stare was cold and unflinchingly blank.

"And I don't think we can just sweep it all under the rug and pretend that we're doing great," I continued. "Do you remember the last time we sat here on this shore? It was when you proposed. You knelt down on one knee and declared your love in exchange for mine. For life! And I couldn't have been more willing than to give it to you. So, what happened?

Something changed over the course of a few months that has created the distance we're feeling today. And I'm going to be honest with you and share what happened on my side of things . . ." I looked to the ground and picked up a shell that glistened in the sun. I threw it toward the ocean and buried my face between my knees. "I met someone else."

His arms recoiled from the sides of my legs and dropped into his lap.

"What?"

"It was after Officer Black's meeting. I was overwhelmed with Emma's disappearance and decided to take a drive up the coast. The trip was stressful, and I wound up stopping at an unfamiliar turnout to gather my thoughts. I noticed there was a trail that led to the beach and thought a little walk would be refreshing. And that's when I met him. I showed no interest in having a conversation and even tried to walk away. But the day was getting late, and I needed to climb a steep trail to get back to my car. He claimed he knew the area well and offered to follow me in case I needed his help. I didn't want to risk getting hurt, so I agreed. I didn't even say goodbye when I got to my car . . ." I paused to allow for him to interject, but he remained quiet.

"I never expected to see him again. It was a simple act of kindness committed by a random, passing stranger. But that wasn't the last time I saw him. He was the person who saved me when I almost drowned."

"And you call him a random stranger? Sure. It sounds like you guys exchanged phone numbers before you got back to your car. Did you tell him you were going to the beach so he could meet you there?"

"No. I know it sounds really weird, but he had no idea where I was," I lied. "He just happened to be there when I fell into the water. And I was thankful that he was, otherwise I wouldn't be sitting here right now. Besides, I would've never fallen off those rocks if we had met like we were supposed to. He was there for me when I needed someone. And you . . . well, you were nowhere to be found."

"But I thought I told you where I was on your birthday. I was looking for your gift, and I didn't—"

"No, that's not what I'm talking about. He was there for me emotionally when you checked out. I was misled into believing he was right for me because he filled a void that you created. I was hurt, and I needed someone's attention badly. You can't blame me for wanting that, right?"

He sputtered out his breath and pushed at the sand with his palms. My eyes fixated on the pink horizon while I waited for him to respond.

"I checked out emotionally because you were already gone. You were gone when Emma disappeared. And things only got worse as time progressed. I didn't know who you were becoming, and I didn't know how to cope with the results. I guess I did what anyone else would've done in the situation, and I withdrew. It's easier to deal with rejection if you don't really care if it happens. And as far as I was concerned, you were falling out of love with me."

I turned at the change in his voice and melted at his expression. Sadness was evident in his eyes before his hair fell forward and covered them completely.

"Oh, Ryan! I wasn't falling out of love with you. I was puzzled by your behavior and adopted some of that mentality myself. I was vulnerable and became distracted by this other person. But nobody could ever take your place. And it took me losing our relationship to realize that. No matter how many fights we get into or how many difficulties we face, our relationship will always be irreplaceable." I brushed away the sand from his stiff hand and rubbed it against my cheek. The feel of his skin against mine made me shudder in remorse.

"I never want to lose you again," I whispered. "This whole nightmare has been one really big misunderstanding."

He sat there quietly as I massaged both of his hands in mine. I was hoping the harder I massaged, the more he would realize I was truly genuine.

"So . . . did you do something with this guy?" he muttered, warming to my touch.

"Only a brief kiss. But as I said before, this person means nothing to me." I wrestled within my heart as the memories of that night suddenly threatened to resurface.

"Ugh, Gwen! Why did you have to go and do something with him?"

I remained completely still as I expected to be flung to the sand and abandoned in rejection. But a sudden feeling of warmth circled around my shoulders. He pulled me to his chest and embraced me from behind. The unexpected act of forgiveness made me want to cry.

"So, you forgive me then?" I asked weakly.

"Yes, I do. We all make mistakes. I can't hold anything against you. I've learned a lot in the time we were apart. I can't fight against something that makes me uncomfortable. I need to learn to accept it for what it is. If I recognized your grief for Emma's disappearance, we wouldn't be having this conversation right now." His eyes pinned on the gray waters that spilled before us. "Our lives are a lot like this ocean," he pointed out. "They're continually changing. We need to adapt to the current and not fight against it. The more we resist the change, the more we'll get pommeled to the floor."

In his brief explanation of life and lessons, I heard all I needed to hear. We both made mistakes in the past. And we both needed a chance to forgive. There was no need to pry about women or mermaids because I had another relationship myself. But I was confident that he didn't cheat. I could feel it in his touch.

"So, what was this guy's name anyways?"

"His name is Marcus."

***

I unzipped the duffle bag on my bed and began stuffing the contents quickly inside. A woman's sweatsuit in size medium, a hairbrush, flip-flops, a mirror, a bath towel, and a set of keys to my apartment. I checked my list one last time and threw in a bottle of water just in case. Avangeline had all she needed to enter society with modesty and restraint. Although knowing her, she'd walk the streets of GlenPoint naked if it meant she'd get to use her legs. She was going to have a hard time fitting into society. Her road was an uphill battle—one she could fight herself. Yes, I finalized our agreement and would offer my apartment until she got a place of her own. But my concern really wasn't for her. Gwendolyn was the real reason I was going tonight. I wanted to be there for her when she realized Ryan was not. I wanted to hold her hand and declare a love that would never waver. Perhaps the sight of Ryan's death would be troubling, and she would need my comfort. But the chances of that happening were highly unlikely. She invited him to the beach knowing what repercussions would happen. And no one would deliver a loved one to be killed. I glanced at the alarm clock on my nightstand and gave the zipper a hard tug.

Eight twenty-eight.

The party started nearly three and a half hours ago. I needed to hurry if I wanted to make it there in time—if I wasn't too late already. I slung the strap over my leather-clad shoulder and headed for the door.

***

An unexpected breeze ripped through the shores of GlenPoint as the night's harsh chill began to set in. The miserable gusts of wind were strong and icy, and if it wasn't for the dwindling embers of our smoking campfire, the conditions would make enduring a party nearly impossible. But the sudden change of weather didn't deter the spirited guests. The howling of the wind and the distant roar of waves only set a perfect stage for three budding couples that longed to flourish. Joey and Jessica exchanged high-pitched giggles as she combed through the tangles in his unbraided hair. Bryan and Alice discussed what colleges they were planning to attend while they cuddled under a large fleece blanket. And Dallas and Ayesha lay locked in a passionate kiss, rolling across the sand. After a long conversation and a well-needed walk, Ryan and I returned to the party in amazement to discover what transpired in our absence. It took Ryan a convincing minute of observation before he commented on his friends.

"Well, will you look at that? The boys finally became men. I hate to admit it, but there was always a sense of superiority to be the only one in the group with a girlfriend. Now I have to listen to all the made-up locker-room stories and give advice about messy breakups. Ugh! Now I have to put up with all the annoying company if the girlfriends decide to come along on our outings. What did I get myself into by having this party?"

Another breeze struck the shore hard, sending a mist of saltwater and grit across my legs. I fought to maintain my endurance for the conditions, but nothing worked. One hand held my flapping dress down while the other blocked the chill from invading my chest. The air was so cold that my body began to tremble.

"What happened to Lindsey?" I asked through chattering teeth.

Ryan broke from his stare and noticed my miserable plight. He quickly untied his sweatshirt from around his waist and draped it across my shaking shoulders.

"Oh, Gwen! You're freezing. Why didn't you tell me you were so uncomfortable?"

"I don't know. I left my sweater in the truck. But I wasn't expecting for the weather to change so quickly. I can go run and get it if you'd like."

He looked back at his preoccupied friends and shook his head with resolve. "No. There's no use. This party's over. I can't get the guys to talk to me right now if I paid them. And why stay here and be miserable when we can go someplace to get warm and comfortable? How does a cup of coffee and a movie sound? If we slip away right now, we can prevent the guys from finding out and avoid any irritating tagalongs they might want to bring. It will be just you and me," he said, looking down into my eyes. "Just like old times."

The greater part of my heart rejoiced upon hearing his suggestion. Our relationship was struck down, but not completely destroyed. We were going to share an evening without any awkward pretenses or feelings of mistrust. It was just him and me and the love we shared.

Just like old times.

"Oh, that sounds great," I said, smoothing back my hair that blew across my face. "I can think of a few good movies that are playing right now. Besides, anything's better than staying out here and freezing to death."

"Good. It's settled then. I'll walk you back to the truck, and you can start the heater. Don't worry about the cooler. I'll go get our stuff."

His warm fingers wove between mine as we crossed through the unaware party to the parking lot. I slid onto the cold seat and rubbed my hands together for warmth.

"Here," he grunted, leaning over my lap to start the engine. "Turn the heater on full blast. It should take the engine a second or two to heat up. But you'll be feeling great in no time. I'll go and attempt to pry the lovebirds off the blanket. Now don't turn into a popsicle on me." He gave my cheek a quick peck and closed the door on the pestering wind.

I stretched my feet to the floorboards and sought the heater's warmth. It began to heat up and liven my frigid extremities. I pulled my sweater over my head and looked at the ocean that was clothed in shadows. A final glimpse of Ryan glowed under a full moon before he crossed over the hill and disappeared completely. I smiled and looked back at the dashboard with relief.

He made it!

He made it through the whole party without even a wayward glance at the ocean. He never made any unusual comments. He never took any unexplained trips. He never even used the restroom. He remained in eyesight the whole time while staying true to our relationship. So much for Marcus and his story of mermaids. If anyone was unfaithful in our relationship, it was me. And Avangeline said it would take only one more encounter to take his soul. What a farce! I was a fool for believing in such a scam. Why did I set up this party in the first place? Did I really expect to see him in the embrace of some creature? I looked back to the ocean and saw his tiny form appearing over the sand dune, cooler in tow.

How faithful he turned out to be. And to think he was hiding an affair. I suppose I needed to disclose the rest of Marcus's story and the real reason why I chose to have a party. But that would have to come at a later date. There was no use in spoiling the night now.

A loud bang sounded from the back of the truck, followed by the scraping of metal. He slid the cooler deep inside and slammed the back door shut. Instead of joining me in the driver's seat, he walked to the side of my window and motioned for me to roll it down.

"Hey, listen," he breathed, sounding slightly winded, "I could be wrong, but I think I saw Joey noticing when I grabbed the cooler. I know we planned to leave without saying goodbye, but that would be kinda rude. Right?"

"Yes, you're right. It would be rude because we were the ones who hosted the party. And Jessica did us a favor by inviting her friends to come. It would be only fair to leave the party on a positive note. Yes, you're absolutely right. Go tell them the weather got too cold for us to hang out. And please say goodbye from me, too. Okay?"

"Sure thing. And, hey, leave the car running. This shouldn't take long."

***

The destination of where I was going was certain, but my passageway there was flawed. I've been on the road for nearly twenty minutes and only progressed a few blocks from my apartment. Between buses, cars, and pedestrians wanting to cross, it felt as though every force was against me from getting to my objective. And it took every ounce of willpower not to jump out of my skin and scream at them all. My fingers tapped nervously on my steering wheel while a slow-moving vehicle merged into my lane. It swerved to the gutter and braked as a younger couple waved from the opposing sidewalk. I quickly peered over my shoulder in a desperate attempt to pass it up. The lane that held my ticket to freedom stretched bumper-to-bumper with endless traffic. Seconds seemed like hours, and after an eternity of waiting for my opportunity to merge, a bus allowed for me to enter, and I quickly pulled in behind it. But no sooner did my car pick up speed when a string of taillights signaled for yet another red light. I hesitantly took the stoplight's suggestion and came to a complete stop. I balled my hand into a tight fist and punched it hard against my dashboard.

Hell's fire!

I knew better than to take GlenPoint Strip on a bustling Friday night. Every man, woman, and child was driving in the same direction I was. All the restaurants were packed. Every movie theater had lines. There was no way I was going to make it to the party on time. What on earth was I thinking to leave my house so late? At this rate, it would be faster for me to park my car on the side of the road and walk the whole way there. I glanced at the clock that glowed in the darkness and wiped the sweat that collected on my brow.

Eight fifty-two.

If Ryan was going to meet with Avangeline, he would've done so by now. And I was too far from their location to use any common influence. I had to think of a faster way to get to the beach!

My mind searched for answers as the bus stopped and emptied its travelers. Side streets weren't as fast as traveling on GlenPoint Strip. They were unfamiliar to my knowledge and were riddled with stop signs. But very few people used the back roads since all the tourist attractions were located in the city. And anything was faster than being trapped behind a bus.

With an alternative route firmly in place, I changed the direction of where I was headed and made a hard right at the nearest intersection. A chorus of annoyed car horns blared from behind me as I sped my way down the dark, inconspicuous alley. Brick buildings and dumpsters blurred from my vision while I approached the large parking lot at illegal speed.

I didn't get excited when I saw the beach's shore. I knew I wasn't anywhere near lifeguard station twelve. The question of how far I really was remained glaringly uncertain. I stopped at the blacktop that was barred off with gates and scanned the gray sand that descended into nightfall. A sign that was posted on a small wooden outlook made my heart sink with anticipated despair.

Lifeguard station thirty-two.

I still had a long way to go. Their party was at least six blocks from where I lingered. But the street that headed in that direction was stoplight-free and clear of buses. With determination in my heart and a prayer on my lips, I set my sights on where I was headed and floored my gas pedal the whole way there.

Thirty-one . . .

Thirty . . .

Twenty-nine . . .

Chapter Thirteen

Ugh!

I couldn't get comfortable. Either I was seeking the warmth that wafted from the floorboards, or I was detesting the stuffiness that it created. The heater that hummed in Ryan's truck had an uncanny way of magnifying my frustration. But seventeen minutes of waiting in a car would make anyone's patience stretch paper-thin. I fidgeted. I shifted. I listened to some music to get my mind off things.

Nothing.

The hill that promised Ryan's return remained completely vacant of any human form. And not only was the hill vacant, but the parking lot was emptying as well. Sometime within the last few minutes, Dallas and Ayesha left the party. It made my blood boil to think of Ryan chatting casually with his friends while I sat and waited for his arrival. I pulled off the sweater that itched around my neck and threw it to the floor.

Why would he tell me he would be right back and not hold true to his word? Didn't he remember we were supposed to see a movie? The later the night got, the fewer options we had to see something good. Not to mention my curfew that would inevitably be broken.

Nine o' two.

I didn't want to start the night off like this. We were going to have fun and wipe the slate clean, not soil our fresh start with some unnecessary discourtesy. How difficult was it to excuse oneself from a conversation to include the fiancée whom you left in a car? At least tell me to recline my seat so I can get comfortable! And what was there to talk about anyways? It's not like he hasn't seen his friends all week and has so much to catch up on. And even if that were the case, he should still come and get me.

I wiped away the moisture that collected at my window to get a better look at the shore. My eyes scanned nervously for any flicker of hope before drifting back to the dashboard.

Nothing.

It's been a full twenty minutes, and he was nowhere to be seen. The predicament I suddenly found myself in seemed vaguely reminiscent of the ones I had experienced in the past. Unanswered phone calls. Numerous absences. A missed birthday. All at once, the fears of Ryan's infidelity came flooding back. Suppose he wasn't saying goodbye to his friends. Suppose he was wandering in places he shouldn't— with people he shouldn't.

Nine o' seven.

Our relationship was going to have a tough road ahead if I couldn't trust him to be a little late. I didn't want to question every time he took an extra five minutes to use the bathroom. I wanted to have a measure of trust for unexpected circumstances such as these. Unfortunately, my reserves of confidence have been entirely depleted by his continual missteps and bad decisions.

Nine o' nine.

I was going to give him six more minutes. If he wasn't back by nine-fifteen, I was going to march over that hill and drag him back myself! And at that point, my anger would be justified. No one should take half an hour to say goodbye. Making me wait this long was completely absurd.

Nine-eleven.

I had to think of what I was going to say when I approached him with his friends. I didn't want to come off sounding cross. The last thing I needed was to hear Joey's jokes about having a short temper.

Nine-thirteen.

How rude could someone get? Two minutes shy of half an hour? Really?

Nine-fourteen.

I held my breath and fixed my eyes on the dark, sloping peak. I didn't blink. I didn't move. I waited anxiously for his return. My lungs burned, but I refused to breathe.

Nothing.

And that was it.

I grabbed my sweater from the sand-encrusted floorboard and turned off the engine. I held my hand on the ignition and debated to take his keys. Suppose we missed paths walking, and he needed a way to get inside. I left the keys on the top of his dashboard and slammed the door behind me.

The night's unendurable wind had died to a cool, gentle breeze. It fanned my fuming temper while I approached the party in question. Four shadowed figures stood huddled around a glow of coals, having a conversation. The closer I got, the more I realized who was there. Joey held Jessica around the waist as he talked to Bryan, who was hanging on to Alice.

Ryan was nowhere to be seen.

I mustered all the strength I had left and gave them a weak smile.

"Hey! Look who's coming back for more. Couldn't get enough of our company, eh, Gwenny?" Joey called out from across the sand. He leaned into the side of Jessica's neck and gave her a loud kiss.

I averted my eyes from the lust-filled couple to see if I could spot Ryan. After seeing he wasn't there, I met the four inquisitive stares with a painfully forced chuckle. "I wish that were the case. But I wanted to apologize for not saying goodbye earlier. Ryan and I would've stuck around longer, but the wind made things really uncomfortable. Thank you for coming tonight. It really means a lot to me that you're all here."

"Well, thank you for inviting us. If I hadn't come today, I would've never met this gorgeous woman by my side," Joey gushed, pulling Jessica in for another kiss. She returned his gesture with sickening enthusiasm and pulled her face away.

"That's okay, Gwen," she answered between pecks and giggles. "You didn't have to come back to tell us that. Ryan said you were cold and were getting warm in his truck. He thanked us for coming and said you did, too."

I suddenly felt guilty for not parting on a better note. The real reason I returned wasn't to say some formal thank you, but to inquire about where Ryan really was. I needed to cut the conversation short and casually mention my concern. "Well, the next time I decide to have a party, you guys will be first on the list. And, hey, speaking of Ryan, you guys haven't seen him lately, have you?"

"No . . ." Alice paused, considering my question, "Ryan came here to say goodbye. But that was like fifteen minutes ago. He did mention he needed to use the restroom. Maybe you could find him there?"

The restroom! That was it! No wonder he was taking so long to return.

"The restroom? How could he be using the restroom? The beach's security closed that building at dusk," Bryan commented.

"Well, Bryan, haven't you ever heard of a camper's toilet?" Joey teased.

"A what?" Jessica laughed.

"A camper's toilet. You know . . . you find a shrub that hides your goods and let it all hang out."

"Joey!" Jessica yelled, pushing him on the shoulder. "Don't tell me you've ever done that before. Have you?"

"Uh . . . well, yeah, maybe. Okay, I have. But only once or twice."

The group echoed with laughter as I looked at the parking lot uncomfortably. The restrooms were located a few paces from where we were parked. If Ryan finished using it, he would've undoubtedly noticed I wasn't in the car. That would send him looking for me and complicate matters even worse. I needed to get back to the parking lot as soon as possible.

"Well, I'm sorry to cut things short. But I really need to find Ryan. Thank you for coming tonight. I hope you all had a good time."

"Oh, we did. Thank you. And, hey, be careful of bushes that move," Joey warned from behind me. "You never know what you might find in them."

I knew as I walked to the small concrete building that Ryan wasn't there. But the optimistic part of my brain sent me to its entrance. I grasped the door's heavy handle and gave it a hard tug. It wouldn't budge. Just as Bryan had mentioned, the security locked the restrooms at dusk. I turned around and studied the parking lot for any trees or shrubs. There were none tall enough to hide Ryan's form. I glanced back at the truck that glowed under a street lamp. It was empty. The creeping suspicion that followed my trail was now tapping me on the shoulder. And I didn't want to turn around to acknowledge its presence, but I knew I had to.

Ryan was missing.

He wasn't at the party. He wasn't using the restroom. And he wasn't in the truck. He had completely vanished from this location without notifying me as to where. All impatience that fueled my raging frustration was suddenly replaced with fear. I was helpless. We rode to the party together, and we had plans afterward. The feeling reminded me of waiting for my mother to pick me up from kindergarten. She was late, and I was the last one left to go home. The longer she took to arrive, the more the butterflies stirred in my stomach. I never thought I would feel those feelings again. But here I was, wringing my hands in a very similar situation. Why was he forty-five minutes late and counting? Either he was deliberately meeting with someone else, or something truly was wrong. And it was hard for me to believe that he would squeeze in a rendezvous before going on a date with his fiancée. The timing was just too inconvenient. He left me in the car and told me to keep it running!

Unsure of what to do next, I scanned the perimeter of the building one last time and headed for his truck. Many times, I was told if I ever got lost to stay in one place and wait to be found. He would have to return to the parking lot at some point in the night. If his absence exceeded more than an hour, I would notify the group of his disappearance and call the authorities. The complicated predicament left me no other choice.

A voice suddenly cut through my thoughts and stopped me dead in my tracks.

"Go to the tide pools. The ones where I saved you on your birthday. Ryan is there."

The unexpected breach of privacy sent gooseflesh down my arms.

Marcus was here.

And he knew where Ryan was.

Instinctively, my legs started running in the direction of my command without a second thought. Although my eyes saw where I was going, I couldn't see. Although my feet moved at a frenzied pace, they were planted firmly on the sand. It was as if I were suspended in time, in a blinding haze of questions that were billowing in from every corner. Was he with Avangeline? Did she already kill him? Or was Marcus the one whom I should be fearing? What if Marcus was overcome with jealousy and was planning to attack Ryan?

What if Marcus was planning to kill me? My body went through the motions of running while my mind absently took me all the way to the horseshoe cluster of rocks. I fell to my knees and wheezed when I reached the dark, craggy wall. My lungs burned with fire. My body shook with fear. I didn't want to see what was behind the merciless veil. I didn't want to know the truth.

I slowly crawled to a crack between two large rocks and peered through to the other side. At first, I saw nothing.

Waves.

Foam.

Sand.

Her.

I saw the most captivating creature slither from the edge of the water and disappear from my view. I inched my way closer to the rock until my face was actually touching its wet surface.

I couldn't believe what I was seeing!

The top half of a woman's body joined to the tail end of a fish! It was like the pictures I've seen in fairy-tale books, only she was simply breathtaking. I couldn't take my eyes off the incredible anomaly. Creamy white skin transitioned to pale green scales that glittered like mirrors in the moonlight. Fiery red hair fell to her back in curls, partially covering her flawlessly formed body. Her face was that of an angel's—innocent in expression, yet beautiful to behold. Delicate, fanning fins propelled her body through the sand in a smooth and graceful motion. She slithered from the foaming line of surf to join Ryan, who was standing a few feet away. Her strong, thick tail mounted her body high, like a cobra lifting ready to strike. She wrapped her arms around his waist and pulled him in for a hug. His eyes scanned the beach nervously before he softened in her embrace and gave her a warm smile.

"Oh, Ryan! Where have you been? You said you were going to meet me here three days ago. You know how I wait for you night after night." Her lips pursed to a full pout, giving her face a look of total rejection. "You're beginning to make me feel like you're losing interest." She crossed her arms across her chest and turned to give him her back. He reached for her elbow, but she refused to turn around.

"Avangeline, you know how much I love you. I feel awful I couldn't've met with you sooner. Things have been really difficult for me at home, and I couldn't find the right moment to slip away. But I'm here now with you, right?"

As if his scanty excuse struck some magical chord, she spun around to face her admirer, all dejection forgotten. His narrowed eyes took in her body as he swept away a piece of seaweed that covered her shoulder.

"So, what brings you here tonight? Besides wanting to see me, of course. Did you have plans with your friends or something?" Her carefully planned interrogation hit conviction's nail right on the head. His eyes avoided hers before gradually falling to the sand. She immediately detected his guilty hesitation and reacted with a performance of theatrical jealousy. "Did you have plans with your friends tonight? Don't tell me you had plans with her!"

He spread his hands in silent affirmation, never once looking up from the ground.

Her face reddened with anger. "You didn't break things off with her yet? No wonder you haven't found the right moment to slip away! You're still spending time with your girlfriend. Or should I call her your fiancée? I don't know why I come out here to meet you, Ryan! You say you love me. You say you want to be with me forever and look past the differences that make me unique. But I think you said all those things in haste. I was warned not to give my heart away to a human. I hate to admit it, but I'm afraid I've made a big mistake."

"No! Avangeline, wait! Please!" He reached for her arm to keep her from turning back around. "It's not what it looks like. I don't love Gwen anymore. We're still together, but not because I love her. It's hard for me to break things off with someone I've been with for so long. I don't want to hurt her feelings, and—"

"But hurting mine is any easier? What does my love mean to you? I've been able to accept your relationship, despite the fact that you're still engaged. I gave my heart to you because you promised to give me yours in return. And now this? You can't break up with your fiancée because you don't want to hurt her feelings? Well, if you can't break things off with her, then you can have her! I'll go back to my home where my kind will love and accept me for who I am."

"Avangeline, please! Wait! I love you. I've always loved you."

"You mock me when you say those things."

"No! I'm serious. You have to believe me. I love you with my whole heart. In fact, I've never loved anyone else like this before."

"Then prove it! Prove you love me with your whole heart. Prove I can trust to wait for you in an ocean that doesn't allow for any communication. Prove I'm not wasting my time!"

"But how can I? Aren't my words enough?"

"No, they're not. People speak a lot of things in the moment. I need to know you love me in a way words can't express. I need to feel your affection in touch, not just in empty phrases repeated like a parrot. Kiss me, Ryan!"

"Kiss you?"

"Yes. Kiss me. And not just any kiss. Kiss me with every ounce of your being. And I will be yours for the rest of your life."

The air around me suddenly grew still. The whole time I watched Ryan's affair, I watched as an innocent bystander. His unfaithfulness was something I was unearthing, and there was a legitimate allotment for necessary processing. But the night's arresting development had all at once become a liability. I couldn't pretend the couple would kiss and part ways on good terms. If Ryan chose to kiss Avangeline, it would most certainly result in his death. And even though I hated him for cheating, and the thought of him abandoning me made my blood boil in my veins, I had a responsibility to prevent such occurrences from happening. I needed to jump out from my hiding place and scream for him to stop from the top of my lungs. I needed to throw a rock, or cough, or pretend to stroll in and interrupt their meeting. But the corruption within my heart caused me to stand still. It was the appalling part of my being that stopped and looked at a car crash instead of averting my eyes and driving past it. I just stood there and watched as he wrapped his arms around her body and pulled her in for an embrace.

At first, it was an ordinary kiss. His moaning could be heard as she ran her fingers through the back of his hair. Her hands slipped from his head to his shoulders, where they caressed his back with unbridled desire. He visibly enjoyed the affection she was giving him, and it lasted for nearly two minutes. But when he decided to pull away, he found he was unable to do so. He gave little resistance to the continual draw of her mouth and succumbed to the lust that groped at his will. Her tail wrapped tightly around his legs while his hands pawed greedily at her skin. She caressed, and he groaned, and for another few minutes his love was reciprocated in a moment of ecstasy.

Eventually, it was time for the kiss to come to an end. Ryan found again that he was unsuccessful in parting. His mouth, once willingly covering hers, was locked in a grip he couldn't break. I clasped my hand over my mouth and bit down hard in unspeakable horror.

He began to panic.

He pushed at her body with both hands. He scratched. He pounded. He took a fistful of her hair and tried ripping her head away from his. But Avangeline stood with a frightening tranquility, her composure unshaken by her victim's sudden terror. She never flinched. She never moved. She never opened her eyes. Her hands that caressed the length of his back fell to her sides in comfortable deportment. His frantic movements continued to escalate, like a well-skilled fighter with no sense of direction. He had taken the steps to hell and was unable to escape his death that awaited.

And then . . . there was silence. The tireless spirit that remained within his being subsided and stopped to a nauseating calm.

I pulled my hand away from my mouth and vomited the contents that rushed to my throat. There was a sound that echoed within my ears that would haunt me for the rest of my life.

A crackling sound.

Similar to a piece of firewood when it is consumed by a fire, Ryan's body began to crumble as it slowly deteriorated from a lack of a soul. His face, once flush and full of life, withered to an old man's and drained of all color. His legs buckled beneath him. His arms fell limp at his sides. His body wasn't recognizable as a human's anymore. It was a husk. A mere shell. A dry well used up to one's content and drained of all its worth. His lifeless body fell from her mouth in a pile of dust and crumpled clothing. The casualty that resulted from the need of the moment had little effect on the creature's seared conscience. She opened her eyes with a triumphant sneer and wiped her mouth with the back of her hand. She then looked down at the rubbish in her shadow and whipped back her tail high above her head. With one strong swipe, she flung his clothes across the sea, sending a spray of ash and sand in its wake. Immediately, a wave washed over the incriminating evidence and carried it out to waters unknown. With a kiss on the mouth and a swing of a tail, Ryan's existence was totally obliterated in a matter of a few minutes.

I released the sand I was unknowingly clutching and fell to the floor on shaking heels. I was dirty. My hair stuck to the sides of my head. My legs were covered in sand. My dress smelled like vomit. But no amount of exterior grime could compare to the filth that was discovered within my heart.

How could I just sit there and watch him die?

Why didn't I stop it from happening? I couldn't understand the depth of my own actions. I would help a stranger if they were in trouble—let alone a loved one! So many nights I've dreamt of being in perilous situations, only to wake up and discover it was all just a nightmare. But this was real. And my sudden paralysis to help him escape couldn't be attributed to a night's cold sweat, but to a wickedness of heart that resided deep within my being. I was just as demented and brutal as the venomous demon who killed him.

I looked back at Avangeline, who was propped very still before a rumbling ocean. Her face had a look of total serenity as she patiently waited for her transformation to occur. Her tail flapped softly against the sand, mimicking the repetitive motion of the rolling waves. Every once in a while, she would look down at her waist to inspect its appearance and then back to the water that covered her path. Minutes of watching and waiting went by, and the anticipated moment seemed never to arrive.

All at once, her body seized stiff in a very rigid position, and she fell to the ground in agonizing pain. She stifled a scream with the back of her hand as her tail uncontrollably bucked and quivered. A tear started at the middle of her fins and continued upward until it reached the lower half of her waist. The narrow split bled as it widened and divided, and for a near second, it appeared as though she had two tails thrashing about. Scaled flesh bulged on the sides of her spine, and the curve of human thighs rapidly took shape. Scalloped fins became feet. Smooth muscle became knees. Light green scales vanished to porcelain white skin that glowed like opals under a starlit sky. The mystery of a beginning unfolded before my very eyes in an awe that transfixed the stage on the beach.

A beautiful woman lay naked on the shore.

She remained completely motionless. For the exception of heavy breathing that could be seen from my vantage point, she appeared as though she had fallen into an unconscious state. A large wave washed in and touched the fingers of her outstretched hand. She turned her head to one side and blinked several times. Her body stirred slightly. After a few minutes of immobilization, she propped herself up on shaky arms and lifted to a slumped sitting position. At first, her expression showed no recollection, as if she were unaware of the gift that had just been given. But then, she looked down at her two new appendages and her mouth opened wide to a joyous smile. She no longer suffered the abnormality that made her different from the rest.

She was human.

With eyes wide in wonder, she reached out to touch the length of one leg, inspecting it closely for every curve and crevasse. It was like watching a blind person receive their sight after a lifetime of deprivation. From the tops of her knees to the bottom of her toes, all flesh was explored with great enthusiasm and was appreciated for the miracles they produced. After a careful inspection of both prized limbs, she let out a cry that echoed across the beach and jumped to a stand in surprising elegance. There was no stumbling over unskilled feet or struggles to find the right steps. Avangeline moved with the grace of a doe as she glided across the sand on two slender legs.

She focused on a location close to the parking lot and approached a large rock with purposeful intent. A tall individual stepped out from the shadows and set a small duffle bag down at her feet. She quickly unzipped the offering that was presented and began spilling the contents onto the shore. The stranger looked to where I was hiding and stared.

It was Marcus.

"Please don't leave yet, Gwendolyn. I need to talk to you."

I pushed his voice out of my head and stood to my feet in abhorrence. I didn't need to see anymore. He was right about Ryan, and I was wrong. He was a murderer, and so was I. I couldn't say anything to the police lest I incriminate myself of the same accusation. After all, the absence of my actions in this situation was the same as a contribution to the crime. And so, Marcus's purpose was fulfilled. He was safe from the authorities. His friend was now human, and I would be branded as a perpetual liar. I would be hiding in constant fear from the police, Ryan's friends, and my family. I would wear the cloak of shame, and it would clothe me for the rest of my life. I couldn't bear the thought of going through it alone. I didn't even know how I was going to get home from the beach. I considered walking back to the parking lot and shook my head in growing despair. What good would it do to go there? Was I going to get into his truck and drive myself home as if nothing happened? And I couldn't go back to the party without a probable explanation of his absence. Surely enough time has lapsed to cause alarm in even the most laid-back of individuals. Was I going to disclose that he died? And by whom? If so, I needed to whip up a quick batch of tears and prepare to answer a week's worth of questions.

Eyebrows would be raised by my outlandish reports, but at least I wasn't trapped into repeating a lie forever. And the part about me knowing that he would die if he kissed her? Well, that would have to remain a secret. No one needed to know the depravity of my heart. And who knows, maybe everyone would think I was in shock and write off my story as the rantings of a lunatic. That would be ideal at this point. The sudden resolution to face my fears created a deep-seated dread in the pit of my stomach. I knew what I needed to do. I couldn't stand still and debate what I was going to say next. I needed to just do it.

I closed my eyes in forced concentration and conjured a whimper without any tears. I just witnessed my fiancé dying, and by the standards of an outsider, I should be completely mortified by the event. I needed to express more than a dry whimper—I needed to unleash a full-on bawl! An image of Ryan flashed through my mind. He knelt to one knee as he opened a small box under a star-filled sky. His eyes danced with excitement while he slid the ring down my left, out-stretched finger. His face lovingly looked into mine before withering to an old man's and crumbling to the floor. Several burning tears came to my eyes and slipped down the sides of my cheeks.

Now I was ready to face my accusers.

I started walking in the direction of the party and slowly came to a stop. A strong cramp appeared out of the middle of nowhere. I clutched the middle of my waist and groaned in pain. It was unlike anything I've ever felt before, squeezing both sides of my abdomen like a poorly fitted belt. I tried to brush off the bizarre discomfort and took several steps toward the water. The more I went through the motion of walking, the more the aching increased. The feeling intensified as it spread throughout my waist, traveling down both legs to my lower extremities.

I hobbled back to the rock where I hid and propped myself against it for support. Something wasn't right. I could feel it. It wasn't a sensation I was familiar with, like an upset stomach or the beginning of the flu. It was as if thousands of tiny worms had entered the bones of my legs and were wriggling down to the bottoms of my feet.

The feeling was unnatural.

I peered through the crack to where Marcus was standing, halfway expecting to see his icy stare. Perhaps he was angry with me for not wanting to talk and was trying to prevent me from leaving the beach. But he wasn't looking in my direction. He was talking to Avangeline, who was bent upside down drying her hair with her towel. As the two conversed on the shore, I watched silently from my crevasse while my pain amplified with each passing minute.

I slumped back from the rock and moaned. The worms that invaded my limbs had suddenly increased in speed, like a pan of live maggots being placed over a fire. I looked at my thighs that twitched beneath my dress and reached out to touch their surface. I pulled my hand away from my leg and choked on a gasp of terror.

Their movement could be felt from under my skin.

Before I knew what was happening, an unexpected pressure squeezed both sides of my hips, sending me collapsing to the ground in excruciating pain. I opened my mouth to scream, but nothing came out. The compressing force gripped my upper torso, making the simple act of breathing nearly impossible. I kicked my legs wildly in the sand as an invisible vice reached down from the heavens and clamped them together to become one thrashing limb. The compressing of my legs strengthened, crowding them together so tight I thought I would faint.

"He . . . help me," I croaked. The voice that yelled within my head was no more than a dry whisper. The skin of my legs that was red from the pressure began to shade to an unnatural gray. My lungs filled with air, and I let out a blood-curdling scream.

"Help!"

My knees that swelled within my legs popped and deflated to the size of peas. Bruised flesh melded to pale green. Smooth muscle covered the split of my thighs and filled in the gaps between my shins.

"Someone!"

The toes of my feet involuntarily stretched forward, where two bony fins ruptured and broke through. Glistening scales freckled the length of my waist.

"Please!"

The sound of the waves grew louder. The air reeked strongly of salt. The sand that cradled the curve of my body transformed into a pillow of cashmere.

Was this all just a bad dream? I needed to wake up. Wake up, Gwendolyn! Wake up!

As my transformation came to an end, all pain left my body, and I could finally see the reflection of my newly assigned form.

But what image I beheld, I refused to believe.

A greenish-gray tail slapped loudly against the sand as I tried to escape the nightmare within my soul. The beach that surrounded me slowly faded from sight, and darkness crept in from every corner.

Wake up!

The more I struggled to break free, the more the appendage thrashed wildly in the sand.

Wake up! Wake up, you darn fool! Wake up!

And then . . .

Corruption became me, and all went black.

Chapter Fourteen

The first person to cross over the rocks was Marcus. He uttered not a word, but his face spoke volumes. His eyes scanned the ground frantically as if he were searching for the person beneath the disguise. He looked at my face and then back at my tail in a sorrow that was deepening with each confused glance. He wiped away the sweat from his pale, creased brow and looked toward the rocks that towered above my head. Avangeline wove her way through a cleft in the shadows and jumped down from the rocks to join her grief-stricken friend. Her prideful eyes raked my form mercilessly before giving a condescending chuckle.

"What did I tell you, Marcus? Huh? What did I tell you?! Didn't I say humans couldn't be trusted? What a traitor this one turned out to be!" She kicked at the ground with the toe of her sandal, throwing a sheet of sand across my defenseless body. Marcus broke his stare from my sputtering face to glare at his friend with displeasure.

Avangeline continued to speak as if I weren't there. "Does this come as some surprise to you? Don't tell me you didn't use any common influence to see what you were dealing with."

His frowning lips drew a thinner line as he considered the error of his past.

"You never used common influence to see if she loved Ryan? Why?"

His troubled eyes fell from hers and drifted to an ocean that offered no retreat. "Because I didn't want to violate her privacy," he answered finally. "Such things I held in great respect. I wanted to possess a sincere nobility, not bully my way into someone else's emotions. But I never thought she would make a decision so contrary to her heart. If I knew she would do that, I would've never involved her in the first place."

"Well, I guess that's the risk you take when working with a human. One minute they feel one thing, the next minute they feel another. They're as fickle as this ocean before us. But you knew that going into it, didn't you." She pulled back her hair high above her head and wove her thick ponytail into a loose bun. Several pieces fell around the sides of her face, giving her a look that would take women hours to achieve. She bit her lip that was smoother than oil and continued. "And, really, I don't have any complaints. I got my legs and a new start to life. Everything worked out great for me in the end. So, for that . . . well, what do I care what happens to her?" She shrugged her shoulders with indifference and looked to her companion to agree with her logic. She received nothing but a vacant stare. Marcus was engaged in a battle of mind, of what ifs and whys, and decisions of the past.

"But I was so certain she would hate him for his unfaithfulness," he muttered, more to the air than to her. "I can't understand how someone can love someone else without ever receiving love in return. Why would a person knowingly hand over their affection to somebody so . . . so inconsiderate? It doesn't make any sense."

"Well, take your own words to heart and forget about her. You can have any girl in this city with a snap of your fingers. Close your eyes and point to anyone. Do you want her? Done! She'd melt at your feet with the slightest of flattery. So, why get caught up with this ill-bred wretch?" She looked at my face and cursed under her breath. "Maybe you shouldn't settle for a human anyways. They lack the ability to comprehend who we are. They care nothing for the struggles we've faced or for the obstacles we've overcome to get where we are today. We're either gods to be worshiped or monsters to be feared. There's no middle ground with them. You can't tell this thing your secrets and not have her judge you in return. All she knows is what she's been accustomed to. Look to a human when you have a medical condition or need to engage in a business transaction. But when you crave an emotional relationship, consider your own kind. We'll accept you for who you are. There are no facades to uphold or surprises to divulge. It's just you being the man you were always supposed to be. The man that I've known for the majority of my life . . ." she breathed, stepping in closer. "The man that I've known inside and out. The man that I've . . . the man that I've fallen for."

I didn't have to know Avangeline well to see the masquerade had ended. The power-hungry woman who prided herself in control was taking down her city walls to reveal her true self. The real Avangeline was soft and feminine and had a desire for something we all needed in our lives. Love. She studied his expression with vulnerable eyes, revealing the tiniest bit of fear that was associated with such. But Marcus was so engulfed in his own worries that he was oblivious to the exposure of her weakened demeanor. She quickly closed down with a volatile snap.

"You really are a fool for loving a human! Your broken heart is a consequence of your own doing. You should've left her on the rocks to drown!" She turned on her heel with an outpouring of words and walked a few steps from where he stood. Marcus just stood there in bewilderment of his offense.

I lifted my tail to one side and grunted quietly with discomfort. The scales of my body that were moist from the transformation were suddenly feeling dry. Apart from being unwelcome and thoroughly degraded beyond compare, I desperately craved the ocean's water.

"What . . . what happened to me?" I croaked.

The voice that rang out like a siren in the night made both parties spin around in surprise.

"What happened to you?" Avangeline questioned. "You don't know why you're a mermaid? Are you joking?" She strutted back to Marcus and clucked her tongue in amazement. "It's one thing not to use common influence to see if she still loved Ryan. But you didn't tell her what would happen if she chose his fate? Why, Marcus, you really set this one up for failure, didn't you?"

He ran his hand down the side of his neck and turned to walk away.

Avangeline looked back at me and smiled as if she found great pleasure in what she was about to say. "Gwendolyn, I'm so sorry no one took the time to explain things to you. It seems to me that Marcus found it a minor detail to disclose. You are suffering from a rare condition that typically occurs when a crime has been committed. It's a crime that's unlike all others. One that can't be seen with the eyes, but rather a violation that's committed within your soul." She stopped her pacing to relish in my unease.

I studied her twisted expression with a disturbing revelation. Avangeline didn't hate humans. Avangeline hated me. She hated me enough to kill me. But for what? I didn't know.

"It's a condition called the traitor's curse. A type of payback, if you will, for the debtor of the offense in question. And you, my dear, are that debtor!"

Marcus spun around as if he wanted to say something, but Avangeline cut him short.

"You've delivered a loved one to their death! In the words of the species that you once were, you should be called . . . well, a murderer."

Her flippant mention of the word ran a shiver down my spine. It was one thing to contemplate my sin within the privacy of my heart. But to have it publicly exposed was another. I ducked away from her pointed finger and looked to Marcus in sheer desperation. I needed to be comforted. But he offered no refuge. His eyes held mine with great pity before reluctantly falling to the sand. I lifted my head in defiant confrontation and looked Avangeline square in the face. I refused to believe the truth.

"I didn't kill Ryan. I didn't deliver anybody."

"Oh, but you did, Gwendolyn," she corrected. "All trespasses have ways of finding themselves out. You can't deny the motives of your heart. The proof is in your transformation. Why, you are damned with the very life you've freed."

"But, I didn't—"

"Yes, you did! Did you invite him to the beach knowing he would visit me?"

"No. I invited him to the beach, but I didn't know he was cheating. Or at least I hoped he wasn't."

"Did he slip away to do something inconspicuous, and were you suspicious? Maybe even a little excited that he would die for his unfaithfulness?"

"No! I thought he was saying goodbye to his friends. And even when I couldn't find him, I never wanted him to die."

"Perhaps you were watching us from afar? Did you have an opportunity to stop him from kissing me? Or did you just stand there and watch him perish!"

I looked at her face without blinking until her image began to distort. I couldn't admit to it. I just couldn't. The minute I admitted to the truth, it became real. Hot, stinging tears filled my eyes, and I looked to the ground before they fell. My silence elicited a condescending laugh.

"Well, I don't think I need to say anymore now, do I? Enjoy your life as a mermaid. It's an empty, miserable life. Perhaps it will teach you to appreciate what you have . . . and to let go of the things you don't." Her eyes glanced at

Marcus, and she turned to walk away. Her suggestion was not only meant for me but for him to hear as well.

I looked at my tail, which was beginning to sting, and flipped it to the other side. My scales felt tight and dehydrated. The overwhelming need for water was beginning to cloud my thinking.

Avangeline noticed my uncomfortable squirming and gave me the slightest of nods. "At least you wear your form nicely. With fitly spoken words and the right kind of moves, you shouldn't have any trouble entrapping a man."

I followed her eyes to my exposed breasts and scrambled to cover them with my arms. During the process of my transformation, my dress and underwear had slipped completely below my waist. My face burned with embarrassment.

She chuckled softly in amusement. "There's no need for modesty in the ocean, Gwendolyn. Such concepts are foreign amongst animals. Your naked breasts are just as insignificant as a whale's fin or an octopus's tentacle." She gave her hand a wave. "You know, wearing clothing in the water may be a bit cumbersome for you. But it's exactly what I need." She pulled my dress from my tail and held it up to her body. Her face beamed with excitement while she examined the delicate, ruffled garment. "My! What a lovely shade of coral. I sure hope it fits."

An unexpected call in the distance interrupted the shameful moment.

"Ryan? Gwendolyn? Are you there? Ryan? Hey, man! Are you there?"

It was Joey. His voice seemed to come from another world in a different time.

"Gwen? Gwendolyn, are you okay? Gwendolyn?" Jessica yelled.

Avangeline bunched my clothes in a tight ball and stuffed them quickly between two rocks. Her wide eyes darted to Marcus in fear.

"They're looking for Ryan," she whispered. "If they ask her where he is, she will tell them the truth about his death. We have to get rid of her!"

Marcus's eyes narrowed on hers. He stood unresponsive to her command.

The voices of the couple grew closer. "Gwendolyn? Ryan? Are you there? Gwendolyn?"

"Marcus!" she hissed. "Can't you hear what I'm saying? We have to get rid of her. Are you going to just stand there and do nothing?"

His unwavering stare quickly put her in her place. Her pale face flushed in sudden rage. "Fine! I don't need your help anyways. I can take care of her myself. Oh, stop trying to run away, Gwendolyn! It will only make your tail flap harder."

She quickly rolled her sweatpants to the tops of her knees and grabbed me by my arms. Her nails dug deep into my wrists as she dragged me across the rock-studded shore and slapped me hard into the breaking water. I lifted my head just high enough to breathe as a cooling wave washed over my body and soothed my irritated flesh. Avangeline ran from the water to avoid getting wet.

"You better keep quiet when your friends arrive!" she warned over her shoulder. "Unless you want to be on the front page of every newspaper, I suggest you keep your mouth shut!"

I hesitantly took her suggestion and dove deep into the water.

***

Avangeline's willpower was strong, but my common influence was stronger.

"I won't help you take her to the ocean. Let her future determine itself."

Her face twisted in expected rage. *"But I may be questioned for Ryan's death! Don't you care about that? Or are you afraid your beloved will have to face her fate? Forget about her, Marcus! She doesn't love you. I should've killed her when I had the chance!"*

I gave her a stare that pinned her to the ground and told her I wasn't amused. She knew not to overstep her boundaries. Although she was aggressive toward humans and insensitive to my failed relationship, there were lines that she knew she couldn't cross. Her fear of my wrath was greater than any spiteful vengeance. I released my influence in self-control.

"Fine! I don't need your help anyways. I can take care of her myself. Oh, stop trying to run away, Gwendolyn! It will only make your tail flap harder."

She bent over the mermaid, who was overcome with terror, and dragged her unwilling body out to sea. The image of Gwendolyn falling face-first to the ground was an image I would fight hard to forget. Her life would be changed forever. The honest, caring part of her nature, the traits that set her apart from the rest, would ultimately be attributed to her ruin. A mermaid's life would chew her up and spit her out.

She would fall victim to the immorality or be conformed to its image. But she would never be the same.

She dove headfirst into the breaking water just in time to be concealed from visitors. Avangeline ran to where I stood and wove her arm firmly around mine. My skin bristled with contempt as she uttered a laugh of cruel accomplishment and gently caressed the side of my arm. Although I knew her affection was merely for show, there was a measure of truth behind her actions.

The couple appeared over the tall, sandy hill and looked at each other in bewilderment. They were obviously surprised to see us standing there and not the friends they sought in concern. The male with the blue and red hair spoke first.

"Uh . . . hey, guys. We don't mean to cram your space or anything. But have you seen a couple pass through here recently?"

Avangeline's grip grew tighter around my arm. "A couple? I haven't seen any couple. Have you seen anyone, sweetie?" she asked, looking to me to respond. After seeing I wasn't going to reply, she shook her head promptly and answered. "No, I'm sorry. We haven't seen anybody pass through here tonight. Why? Is there something we can help you with?" Her voice cracked, sounding a bit edgy.

"Well, sort of," the female answered. "We thought we heard our friend screaming. She was looking for her boyfriend, and his truck is still in the parking lot. We thought she might be in trouble."

Avangeline's skin grew cold and clammy. She dropped my arm with nervous energy and cackled a fictitious laugh. "Did you say you heard screaming? Oh, I'm sorry to have worried you. That was me screaming for help. My boyfriend and I were playing near the water, and he decided to push me in. I barely ran away from the water before the wave drenched me completely. He knows how I hate getting wet, and yet he still finds it amusing to torture me. You never cease to amaze me with your antics, Tristan."

The couple drank in her lie like a cold glass of water. They looked at each other with an expression of relief.

Avangeline finished her fictional painting with a brush-stroke of empathy. "Anyways, I'll be sure to tell your friends you're looking for them. And, by the way, what are their names in case we come across them?"

"Their names are Ryan and Gwendolyn," the male informed. "Ryan is tall with brown hair and a black shirt. And Gwen has long blonde hair. I think she's wearing an orange, strapless dress. Isn't that right, Jess?" He looked to his companion, who nodded in confirmation. "Yes, it's orange. If you happen to see them, please have them give us a call. And, hey, sorry to have bothered you." He gave Avangeline a second glance that clearly exceeded curiosity.

She immediately detected his lustful stare and stepped forward in shameless confidence. Now that the danger had passed, she needed to make a lasting impression. And this male was obviously vulnerable.

"I can assure you we weren't bothered by your inquiry," she purred. "And, as I said before, we will notify your friends that you are looking for them." She untied the hair that was piled atop her head and let it fall around her pulled-back shoulders. Although she was covered from head to toe in sweats, any man could see that great beauty lay beneath. She casually lifted a little of her sweatshirt to reveal the tiniest bit of a toned stomach. She scratched at an invented itch and lowered her clothes with a seductive smile. The male's wandering eyes were quickly put in place by the female's jealous voice.

"Well, thank you for your concern. We'd better be on our way." She gave her companion an angry glance and then gave his hand a hard tug. He followed her obediently up the hill.

Avangeline waited until they were gone before she turned to me and grinned. "Are you sure you don't want to give us a chance, Tristan? I think we make a cute couple."

I looked at her face that begged for my affection and gave her a halfway smile. She had a lot to learn about humanity. The animal in her nature would hopefully be tamed with time. The challenge wasn't for a mermaid to acquire legs, but to acquire a heart.

She giggled with excitement and tugged on my arm. "I can't wait to see this club you've spoken of. And your apartment! Are you sure I can stay there until I find a place of my own?"

I stared at the water that spread across my vision and concentrated on a small, moving object. Gwendolyn's head could be seen bobbing up and down in an ocean that seemed so very vast. I closed my eyes with growing sorrow and muttered, "Yes. You can stay with me as long as you need to. And I'll show you La Mer first thing tomorrow. Come on, it's getting late. The parking lot is up this way."

I gave Gwendolyn a final glance and led Avangeline through the night.

Keep reading for a preview of the second
book of *The Unspoken Heart* series,

Change of Tides

Chapter One

The tide pulled back from the shadowed sand, leaving a creamy white sheet of glittering foam. My arms propped my body up from the pebbled ground just high enough to rest on both elbows. I looked down at my tail that glistened in the moonlight and gave a cry of despair.

This wasn't real.

It couldn't be. This heavy fish's appendage that descended from my waist wasn't right. It wasn't natural. I was supposed to see legs kick with a thought, not one muscle. How was I supposed to swim? The pulse in my neck swelled hot at the thought.

The voice of Avangeline drove fear even deeper, "You better keep quiet when your friends arrive! Unless you want to be on the front page of every newspaper, I suggest you keep your mouth shut!" Her harsh words were both a plea and a command. My presence at her murder posed an unforeseen predicament. She didn't plan for me to witness Ryan's death. Her whole transformation was calculated. She didn't anticipate I would hide in the cleft of the rocks and watch her transgression play out. Avangeline needed to cover her tracks and get rid of me fast—even if it meant dragging my body to the shore herself.

Another wave came in, spilling water toward her newly acquired feet. She turned on her heel and ran up the hill.

I glanced at the silhouette that loomed near the rocks and swallowed the lump in my throat. Marcus remained motionless as Avangeline joined his side. I needed his help. I needed something. Anything. I needed a solution. I needed a savior to come and rescue me from this watery hell that was to be my future. But I received nothing. He didn't even look in my direction.

"Gwendolyn? Ryan? Are you there? Gwendolyn?" The voices of Joey and Jessica grew louder. My friends didn't know what happened. They were expecting to find Ryan holding me under the stars. They had no idea I was a mermaid and Ryan disintegrated into a pile of ash. The shock of his murder would be parallel to my form.

The thunderous clap of a large wave sounded, and my waist became submerged. For one suffocating moment, I considered a horrifying option. I could drag myself up the shore and flag down Joey and Jessica. I could get their attention by waving my arms and explain all that happened after the party. They would marvel at my appearance and ask a million questions, but they would never accept the reason why I transformed. Their sympathy for my misfortune would instantly become abhorrence.

"Ryan? Gwendolyn? Ryan . . . man, are you there?"

My soul fainted within me. With the utterance of a prayer, I filled my lungs with a thin breath of air and turned to face the ocean that waited. An incoming wave rose high above my head, swirling indigo peaks with white foam. A scream filled my throat as it struck me in the face and pushed me flat on my back.

I entered a world of total darkness.

The light from the moon was instantly smothered by a blanket of water that spread above my face. The thick, gritty current crashed down upon my chest, expelling the little remaining breath that I held. My pulse throbbed hard in my ears as I struggled to break through the ocean's churning surface. The merciless riptide grabbed my body like a ragdoll and sucked me deep into its trenches. Bits of shell and rock tore my skin like glass as I tumbled wildly in the darkness. I kicked at the water in a desperate attempt to swim, but a fish's tail responded to the command. My brain had not yet registered my transformation. A massive muscle pulled hard in my belly, spreading the delicate fins that were attached at its end. With a few strong flaps, I pushed through the rolling waters that collected at the shoreline and propelled straight to the top.

I burst through the surface with a sputtering gasp and fought to catch my breath. In my mind's eye I imagined two legs kicking vigorously in the water—only a greenish-gray tail waved steadily in their place. I ran one hand down the length of my abdomen and flinched. A seamless transition from skin to scale could be felt just above my hipline. The wide, flexing muscle was hard and slightly slippery, swaying with precise calculation to each mental kick. I pulled my hand away from my tail and continued to grope at the water. The confusion of my appendage was more than I could bear.

Acknowledgement of my aberration brought a flood of self-awareness and grief. I glanced in the direction of the shoreline, halfway expecting to see everyone watching me in horror. Marcus and Avangeline were engaged in a conversation with Joey and Jessica. Excuses for Ryan's and my absence would undoubtedly be made. Avangeline would ensure my friends stayed oblivious to our whereabouts. Little did Joey know the very stranger he spoke to was the one who took Ryan's life.

My skin prickled with gooseflesh, and I shuddered at the thought. I could have prevented his death. He was my best friend and my fiancé, yet I let him die without a struggle. So many memories we shared were completely obliterated by one single decision. And what was the motive for my reaction? Anger at his infidelity? Fear of Avangeline's retaliation? Doubt that he would die? I bit my lower lip and moaned in total abhorrence. It scared me to look into the depths of my heart. Not even I understood the choices I made.

I took another look at the conversing crowd and willed to disappear within the shadows. If Joey turned his head, he would find me floating out to sea. Suddenly, my perilous situation became even more complicated. I loathed swimming underwater as much as I hated my aquatic attachment, but I feared my discovery even more. I took in a reluctant deep breath and sank beneath the surface.

The warm water felt thick as I pulled apart its drapes. With a full moon shining brightly in the sky, a creation of infinite splendor was unveiled before me. Tapestries of dark emerald velvet stretched for as far as the eye could see. Its gentle-moving currents stirred up wisps of effervesce, gold and sparkling, as I swam within its wake. I kicked my tail in short bursts of energy to prevent from going too fast. Slowly, I snaked my way through an ocean that was filled with beauty, wonderment, and power. Clusters of black floating seaweed draped like willow branches from the water's swaying surface. A wave pulled and they opened their folds, revealing a network of tiny fish that twinkled in their lengths. I pushed past the tangle of jelly-like ribbons and drifted toward the moonlight. Although I was underwater for only a few seconds, my lungs were completely depleted of air. The desire to breathe suddenly exceeded the fear of being noticed. Without giving it a second thought, I gave my tail a hard flap and quickly made my climb.

I broke through the ocean's choppy surface and gulped desperately for oxygen. A cold wind blew hard across my face, making a deep breath of air difficult to take. I expanded my chest, but received little relief. My throat bulged, and I coughed. It felt as though my lungs were changing, constricting somehow, and becoming unbearably tight.

I smoothed back my hair that whipped across my face and looked toward the shore. Four small figures stood talking in the darkness. Their company was at a greater distance and had become harder to see. A thin wisp of cloud covered the moon, making distinguishing identities of individuals near impossible. But what I was able to see, I was grateful for. I hadn't traveled so far out that I lost touch of what I knew— lifeguard station twelve, my friends who sought my presence, GlenPoint Strip that led to home—my parents.

My parents!

I covered my mouth with my hand and bit down on my palm. My parents—oh, my parents! They would be worried for me by now! Surely the night's hour was well past my curfew. If sleep prevented them from detecting my absence, it would certainly be discovered in the morning. A simple party at the beach would become their worst nightmare. Calls to the police would be nothing more than failed attempts. They would comb the sands of GlenPoint Beach and never know I was there.

They would think I was dead.

I stifled a sob and blinked my eyes, sending two tears streaming down my cheeks. I would never see them again. My father's infectious laughter, my mother's warm embrace, the memories we made as a tight-knit family of three—all were gone in a blink of an eye. Everything I knew and loved was swallowed in an ocean of perpetual torment.

Another gust of wind blew and the air grew uncomfortably thin. The four individuals who lingered on the shoreline had suddenly dispersed to two. Although I felt excluded from their aloof inner circle, I didn't want them to leave. They were all I had left— the last remains of human interaction. My peace rested in the visual of two detached people. Be it Marcus and Avangeline or Joey and Jessica, I feared once they left GlenPoint Beach my sanity would be shaken to the core.

One of them turned in my direction.

I took in a wheezy breath and ducked underwater.

A hard-rolling wave crashed down upon my head, pushing me deeper than I expected. The moon's precious glow had once again vanished, shrouding me in a cloth that was as dreaded and as black as death. I needed to stay out of sight, and I wasn't sure how long. My lungs were already out of air. I fanned my tail with a thought of a kick and slowly treaded in place. The smooth stir of tide pulled my body where it wished as I succumbed to the will of the ocean. I extended my arms at my sides to gain better balance as I floated.

A slippery object brushed against my hand.

I kicked my tail with instinctual force and surged back to the top. I exploded out of the water with a gargled scream and pawed at the waves on the surface. My hand tangled in a spider web of seaweed, pulling the leathery bundle of vines close to my body. I pushed away the plant that wrapped around my arms and steadied my breathing to a pant. My frightening encounter was nothing more than vegetation. The draping clusters of greenery were surrounding me like a fortress of floating walls, making every move in the darkness an accidental run-in. The ocean was such a complex and unforgiving environment. I was fortunate I didn't come across a jellyfish or an eel. Heaven only knew what creatures hid within the depths.

A realization suddenly hit me that I hadn't thought of before. I felt my face drain of all color.

Sharks.

Beasts of vicious enormity dwelled within my living space. I was no longer a human who held power over my circumstances. I didn't have the capacity to get into a boat or swim to safety if danger unexpectedly arose. I didn't have lifeguards manning the shoreline and boundaries for which I knew not to cross. Every flap of my tail lured the monsters from the crevasses. I was vulnerable and exposed, and any movement I made put my life in danger.

My vision pulsed in sync with my heartbeat. With trembling hands, I cleared away the remaining seaweed that clung to my frame and squinted to get a better look at the shore. The last remains of my company had vanished. The sobering perspective their presence provided had abruptly become nonexistent.

All at once, fears crawled out of the rafters of my mind and lined up to be looked over and embraced—Ryan's death and my participation, family and friends whose lives would be shattered by my disappearance, the dangerous environment I was forced to call home, basic tools of life that were lost overnight. Where would I sleep? What would I eat? What would I wear? My naked breasts were just as hard to accept as anything else I had to deal with. The Gwendolyn Hart that once existed, died, and nothing could bring me back from a future that was destined for destruction. Nothing except . . .

Murder.

My soulless body required a sacrifice to receive legs. I needed to lure a man to fall in love with me and give me his life with a kiss. The solution was as frightening as it was cruel. And it wasn't a haste decision. The act needed to be performed slowly and methodically, and every second spent fulfilling my entrapment was a second given for moral reflection. In the end, it was my life for his—an exchange of unjust scales. My side would always weigh out lacking. I would lay in my bed of pillows and cotton sheets and remember the man whose life that it cost. The demons that tormented Marcus's contentment would eventually come knocking on my door. It was a visit I wasn't wanting to entertain.

An image Ryan suddenly conjured in my mind. His blue eyes were ablaze with excitement as he took in every inch of Avangeline. She questioned his fidelity, and he defended his intentions with a pledge of total devotion. After seeing that her victim was ready for the taking, she demanded for his affection with a kiss. He, being smitten with the goddess that beckoned, was only more than willing to oblige. She ran her fingers through his sandy brown hair while he caressed the middle of her back. Their mouths pressed willingly in unbridled desire before he discovered he was stuck and struggled to break free. His taut skin stretched wrinkly. His angular jaw sagged. Both legs wobbled at the knees and buckled. His young, muscular body became shriveled like an old man's as she sucked the very life out from him. He crumpled to the sand in a pile of ash and clothing just in time for a wave to wash him away. The man who ate from the fruit of my seduction would ultimately fall to the sand in eternal ruin.

I closed my eyes and blotted out the image that felt so very fresh. A fine mist of saltwater carried up from the waves, choking my breath that was becoming quite labored. For the first time I noticed how very little input and output my lungs were exchanging. Deep breaths of air felt restricted and lacked substance, and if I received any relief from my feeble efforts, they were entirely depleted the moment I sank underwater.

I opened my mouth as wide as I could and inhaled with a strenuous rasp. A burning pain shot across my chest, and I exploded in a crackling cough. The more I tried to catch my breath, the more the pain spread. I grabbed at my throat to keep from sputtering as my heart began to race.

I couldn't breathe.

No matter how hard I tried, my lungs couldn't fill with enough oxygen. The simple act of breathing that nourished me since birth had suddenly become inefficient. It was as if my body was rejecting the very substance it needed and was requiring something different to live.

A hard-pressing wind beat across the ocean, splashing a wave against my face. I looked at the water that played quietly in the darkness and closed my eyes in despair. My oxygen wasn't coming from the right source. If my legs changed to a fish's tail, it would only make sense that my lungs changed as well. I needed to take a deep breath underwater.

The fiery pain that lingered in my chest spread to the middle of my back. I bent my head toward the glassy black water and lightly touched my lips to its surface. The ocean lapped against my mouth, whispering for me to breathe it in. I made a mental count of three and gave a sharp slurp. A flood of salty liquid shot down the back of my throat, and I gagged at the offering. I could taste blood. My failed attempt to remain alive offered no promise. White dots floated across my vision, and my ears began to ring. The night's starry sky that stretched above my head blended with the innumerable floating spots around me.

I needed to go home.

My sight darkened to black. I turned in the direction of the shore and fanned my tail with the little strength I had left. If I hurried, I could make it back before breakfast. I could drag myself up the shore and wait for someone to see me. They could carry me to their car and drive me back home. Yes! That was my plan. My parents would be so happy to see me that they would embrace my new body. I flapped my tail hard at the thought of their smiling faces and swam as fast as I could. I needed to make haste if I was going to make it back in time.

I just need to go home.

A thick object wrapped around my neck and pulled me underwater.

"Speak your name before I kill you!"

Change of Tides
is now available at https://a.co/d/02wssnBh

Amy Astorga has a passion for unearthing monsters that lurk in the darkness and illuminating their pathways to redemption. Unafraid to take chances, she boldly fuses dark fantasy with powerful, faith-based themes. Her narratives point readers toward a transcendent hope only found in Christ.

When she's not navigating the beautiful chaos of raising six children, Amy can be found collecting perfumes, studying insects, or losing a battle with a never-ending pile of laundry.

Follow amyastorga.com for updates.